50
Great
Bedtime Stories

for 4 to 6 year-olds

First published in 2001 by Miles Kelly Publishing Ltd

This edition published in 2006 by Bardfield Press

Bardfield Press is an imprint of Miles Kelly Publishing Ltd
Bardfield Centre, Great Bardfield, Essex, CM7 4SL

4 6 8 10 9 7 5

Editorial Director: Belinda Gallagher
Art Director: Jo Brewer
Project Manager: Paula Borton
Editorial Assistant: Bethanie Bourne, Isla MacCuish
Production Manager: Elizabeth Brunwin
Reprographics: Anthony Cambray, Stephan Davis, Liberty Newton, Ian Paulyn

British Library Cataloguing-in-Publication Data
A catalogue record for this book is available from the British Library

ISBN 978-1-84236-478-9

Printed in China

www.mileskelly.net
info@mileskelly.net

ACKNOWLEDGEMENTS
David Higham Associates for **The Amazing Talking Pig** by Mick Gowar © Mick
Gowar, **Billy the Kid Goes Wild** by Francesca Simon from *Moo Baa Baa Quack* repro-
duced courtesy of Orion Children's Books, **The Little Boy's Secret** David
L Harrison for permission to reprint fom *The Book of Giant Stories*, 1972, co-published
by Jonathan Cape Ltd (England) and American Heritage Press (USA)
The Wiggly Tooth Copyright © 1997 Dorothy Edwards Reproduced by permission
of the author c/o Rogers, Coleridge and White Ltd, 20 Powis Mews, London W11 1JN.

50 Great
Bedtime Stories

for 4 to 6 year-olds

Edited by Fiona Waters

BARDFIELD
PRESS

Contents

Fairytale Magic

Animals Big and Small

The Moon and Stars and Rainbows

Boys and Girls

Wizards and Witches, Giants and Genies

We have given you an approximate time each story will take to read aloud.

The Magic Porridge Pot	*6 mins*	Snow Daughter and Fire Son	*5 mins*
The Twelve Dancing Princesses	*4 mins*	The Moon Caught in the Marsh	*4 mins*
The Frog Prince	*5 mins*	The North Wind and the Sun	*2 mins*
Cinderella	*5 mins*	East of the Sun and West of the Moon	*9 mins*
Snow White and Rose Red	*5 mins*	The Little Boy's Secret	*5 mins*
Rumpelstiltskin	*5 mins*	The Sorcerer's Apprentice	*4 mins*
The Elves and the Shoemaker	*5 mins*	Goldilocks and the Three Bears	*4 mins*
The Princess and the Pea	*3 mins*	Peter and the Wolf	*3 mins*
The Three Wishes	*3 mins*	The Wiggly Tooth	*6 mins*
Kaatje's Treasure	*4 mins*	Dick Whittington	*5 mins*
The Lion and the Mouse	*2 mins*	The Precious Stove	*7 mins*
Why the Manx Cat has no Tail	*3 mins*	Little Red Riding Hood	*4 mins*
Chicken Licken	*2 mins*	The Gingerbread Boy	*3 mins*
The Three Little Pigs	*4 mins*	Jack and the Beanstalk	*6 mins*
Billy the Kid goes Wild	*3 mins*	Liam and the Fairy Cattle	*6 mins*
Why the Robin has a Red Breast	*4 mins*	Hansel and Gretel	*6 mins*
Androcles and the Lion	*2 mins*	Amal and the Genie	*4 mins*
The Ugly Duckling	*4 mins*	Snow White and the Seven Dwarfs	*8 mins*
The Three Billy Goats Gruff	*4 mins*	The Giant who Counted Carrots	*5 mins*
The Amazing Talking Pig	*9 mins*	The Mermaid of Zennor	*4 mins*
The Greedy Dog	*3 mins*	The Seven Ravens	*6 mins*
The Cat and the Mouse	*5 mins*	The Twelve Windows	*6 mins*
The Star Maiden	*5 mins*	Sleeping Beauty	*5 mins*
How Jumbo went to the Moon	*4 mins*	Rapunzel	*5 mins*
The Lad who went to the North Wind	*4 mins*	Teeny Tiny	*2 mins*

Fairytale Magic

The Magic Porridge Pot

a Swedish folk tale

This is the story of an old porridge pot. One day, just before Christmas, a poor old farmer and his wife decided that they needed to sell their last cow as they had no money left, and no food in the cupboard. As the farmer walked sadly to market with the cow, he met a very strange little man on the road. He had a long white beard right down to his toes, which were bare, and he wore a huge black hat, under which the farmer could only just see the bright gleam of his eyes. Over his arm he carried a battered old porridge pot.

"That's a nice looking cow," said the strange little man. "Is she for sale?"

"Yes," said the farmer.

"I shall buy your cow," declared the strange little man, putting the porridge pot down with a thump. "I shall give you this porridge pot in exchange for your cow!"

Well, the farmer looked at the battered old porridge pot, and he looked at his fine cow. And he was just about to say, "Certainly not!" when a voice whispered, "Take me! Take me!"

The farmer shook himself. Dear me, it was bad enough to be poor without beginning to hear strange voices. He opened his mouth again to say, "Certainly not!" when he heard the voice again. "Take me! Take me!"

Well, he saw at once that it must be a magic pot, and he knew you didn't hang about with magic pots, so he said very quickly to the strange little man, "Certainly!" and handed over the cow. He bent down to pick up the pot, and when he looked up, the strange little man had vanished into thin air.

The farmer knew he was going to have a difficult time explaining to his wife just how he had come to part with their precious cow for a battered old porridge pot.

She was very angry indeed and had started to say a lot of very cross things when a voice came from the pot,

"Take me inside and clean me and polish me, and you shall see what you shall see!"

Well, the farmer's wife was astonished but she did as she was bid. She washed the pot inside and out, and then she polished it until it shone as bright as a new pin. No sooner had she finished than the pot hopped off the table, and straight out of the door. The farmer and his wife sat down by the fire, not saying a word to each other. They had no money, no cow, no food and now it seemed they didn't even have their magic pot.

Down the road from the poor farmer, there lived a rich man. He was a selfish man who spent all his time eating huge meals and counting his money. He had lots of servants, including a cook who was in the kitchen making a Christmas pudding. The pudding was stuffed with plums, currants, sultanas, almonds and goodness knows what else. It

was so big that the cook realised she didn't have a pot to boil it in. It was at this point that the porridge pot trotted in the door.

"Goodness me!" she exclaimed. "The fairies must have sent this pot just in time to take my pudding," and she dropped the pudding in the pot. No sooner had the pudding fallen to the bottom with a very satisfying thud, than the pot skipped out of the door again. The cook gave a great shriek, but by the time the butler and the footman and the parlour maid and the boy who turned the spit had all dashed into the kitchen, the pot was quite out of sight.

The porridge pot in the meantime trotted down the road to the poor farmer's house. He and his wife were delighted to see the pot again, and even more pleased when they discovered the wonderful pudding. The wife boiled it up and it lasted them for three days. So they had a good Christmas after all, while the old porridge pot sat quietly by the fire.

Spring came, and still the porridge pot sat quietly by the fire. Then one day the pot suddenly trotted over to the farmer's wife and said,

"Clean me, and polish me, and you shall see what you shall see."

So the farmer's wife polished the pot till it shone as bright as a new pin.

No sooner had she finished than the pot hopped off the table, and straight out of the door.

You will remember that the rich man was very fond of counting his money. There he sat in the great hall, with piles of golden guineas and silver sixpences on the table, and great bulging bags of coins on the floor at his feet. He was wondering where he could hide the money when in trotted the pot. Now the cook had been far too frightened of the rich man's temper to tell him about the pot stealing the Christmas pudding, so when he saw the pot he was delighted.

"Goodness me!" he exclaimed, "The fairies must have sent this pot just in time to take my money," and he dropped several bags of money in the pot. No sooner had

the bags fallen to the bottom with a very satisfying clink, than the pot skipped out of the door again. The rich man shouted and hollered, but by the time the coachman and the head groom and the stable lad had run into the great hall, the pot was quite out of sight.

It trotted down the road to the poor farmer's house. He and his wife were delighted to see the pot again, and even more pleased when they discovered the bags of gold and silver. There was enough money to last them for the rest of their days, even after they had bought a new cow.

As for the battered old porridge pot, it sat quietly by the fire for many a long year. Then, one day, it suddenly trotted straight out of the door. It went off up the road until it was out of sight, and the farmer and his wife never saw it again.

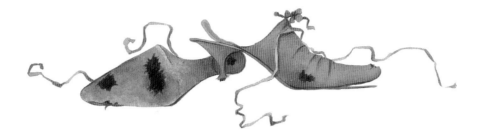

The Twelve Dancing Princesses

a retelling from the original story by the Brothers Grimm

The king was very puzzled. He had twelve daughters, each one as beautiful as the moon and the stars, and he loved them above all the riches in his kingdom. But every morning the princesses would appear yawning and bleary-eyed, and with their shoes worn quite through. Every evening the king would kiss them good night and lock the door behind him. So how did they get out? And where did they go? The princesses certainly were not letting on.

Buying new shoes every day was costing him a fortune so the king determined to solve the mystery. The court messenger was sent to all four corners of the kingdom to issue the king's proclamation that he would give the hand of one of his daughters in marriage to any man who could discover the secret. But should he fail after three nights he would be banished forever.

Needless to say there were plenty of young men willing to risk banishment to win such a prize. But they soon found the princesses were too clever by half. Before they retired for the night, the princesses sang and played their musical instruments and fed them sweetmeats and rich honeyed mead. Before they realised it morning had come and there were the sleepy princesses and twelve pairs of worn-out shoes.

The king was beside himself. Only the court shoemaker went about with a smile on his face.

Now into the kingdom at this time there wandered a penniless soldier. He read the proclamation and had just decided to try his luck when an old woman came slowly down the dusty road. The young man offered her some of his bread and cheese, and as they sat peaceably together the old woman asked where he was bound. When he had explained she said, "Well, I may be able to help you. You must not drink the mead those cunning princesses offer you, for it is drugged. Pretend to be asleep, and you shall see what you shall see. This may help you," and the old woman handed him a silvery cloak. "Whenever you wear this you will be invisible. Use it well!" and the old woman disappeared.

"Well, perhaps I will succeed now I have magic on my side," murmured the young man as he set off for the palace. By now the king was tearing his hair out. The court shoemaker had taken on extra cobblers to help keep up with the demand for new shoes every day. The princesses were falling asleep into their bowls of porridge at breakfast every morning.

The young man bowed deeply to the king and smiled at all the princesses. He ate a hearty supper but when the eldest princess gave him a goblet of mead he only pretended to drink it. Then he yawned loudly and let his head droop as if he had fallen asleep.

The butler and the first footman dumped the young

man onto the bed placed
across the door of the
princesses' bedchamber. He
cautiously opened one eye
and gazed around the
room. The princesses were
putting on gorgeous velvet
and brocade dresses
and rings and
necklaces. They
giggled and
whispered as they
brushed their hair,
powdered their faces
and then pulled on
the brand new
jewelled slippers

that the shoemaker had only delivered a few hours earlier.
The eldest princess clapped her hands three times. A trap
door opened up in the floor and they all swiftly descended
down a steeply curving staircase. Just as soon as the last
princess had disappeared the young man flung the magic
cloak round his shoulders and rushed after them.

He found himself in a wondrous garden where the trees
were covered in rich jewels, sparkling in candlelight.
Musicians played whirling tunes and he saw all the
princesses dancing with the most handsome princes. The

young man was spellbound, but he managed to keep his wits about him. He reached up and broke off a branch from one of the jewelled trees and hid it under his cloak. Then he ran back and lay down on his bed as though he had never stirred. So it happened on the second and the third nights.

It was with a weary voice that the king asked the young man at breakfast on the fourth day if he had found out where the princesses went at night. The king sat up very quickly when the young man told his tale and produced the branches from the trees. The king was delighted and the young man chose the youngest sister for his bride. And they all lived happily ever after. Except, of course, the court shoemaker, who always made the young man's shoes just a little too tight so they pinched.

The Frog Prince

a retelling from the original story by the Brothers Grimm

Once upon a time, there lived a very spoilt princess who never seemed content. The more she had, the more she wanted. And she just would not do what she was told.

One day she took her golden ball out into the woods, although she had been told by her chief nanny that she must embroider some new handkerchiefs. She threw the golden ball high up into the sky once, twice, but the third time it slipped from her hands and, with a great splash, it fell down, down into a deep well. The princess stamped her foot and yelled, but this did not help. So she kicked the side of the well, and was just getting ready for another big yell, when a very large frog plopped out of the well.

"Ugh!" said the princess. "A horrible slimy frog, go

away at once," but the frog didn't move. Instead, it spoke.

"What are you making such a fuss about?"

A talking frog! For a moment the princess was speechless, but then she looked down her nose and said,

"If you must know, my most precious golden ball has fallen down this well, and I want it back."

With a sudden leap, the frog disappeared down the well. In the wink of an eye, it was back with the golden ball. The princess went to snatch it up, but the frog put a wet foot rather firmly on it and said,

"Hasn't anyone taught you any manners? 'Please' and 'thank you' would not go amiss, and anyway I have a special request to make."

The princess looked at the frog in utter astonishment. No one ever dared talk to her like that, and certainly not a frog. She glared at the frog and said crossly,

"May I have my ball back, please, and what is your special request?"

The frog did not move its foot, but bent closer to the princess.

"I want to come and live with you in the palace and

eat off your plate and sleep on your pillow, please."

The princess looked horrified, but she was sure a promise to a frog wouldn't count so she shrugged her shoulders and said, "Course you can," and grabbed her golden ball from under the frog's foot and ran back to the palace very quickly.

That night at supper the royal family heard a strange voice calling,

"Princess, where are you?" and in hopped the frog.

"Oh bother!" said the princess. The queen fainted. The king frowned.

"Do you know this frog, princess?" he asked.

"Oh bother!" said the princess again, but she had to tell her father what had happened. When he heard the story, he insisted the princess keep her promise.

The frog ate very little, the princess even less. And when it was time to go to bed, the king just looked very sternly at the princess who was trying to sneak off on her own. She bent down and picked the frog up by one leg, and when she reached her great four-poster bed, she plonked the frog down in the farthest corner. She did not sleep a wink all night.

The next evening, the frog was back. Supper was a quiet affair. The queen stayed in her room, the king read the newspaper, and the princess tried not to look at the frog. Bedtime came, and once again the frog and the princess slept at opposite ends of the bed.

The third evening, the princess was terribly hungry so she just pretended the frog was not there and ate everything

that was placed in front of her. When it came to bedtime, she was so exhausted that she fell in a deep sleep as soon as her head touched the pillow.

The next morning when she woke up, she felt much better for her good sleep until she remembered the frog. But it was nowhere to be seen. At the foot of the bed, however, there stood a very handsome young man in a green velvet suit.

"Hello, princess. Do you know that you snore?" he said.

The princess's mouth fell open ready to yell, but the handsome young man continued, "I don't suppose you

recognise me, thank goodness, but I was the frog who rescued your golden ball. I was bewitched by a fairy who said I was rude and spoilt," and here the young man looked sideways at the princess whose mouth was still hanging open, "And the spell could only be broken by someone equally rude and spoilt having to be nice to me."

The princess closed her mouth. The king was most impressed with the young man's good manners, and the queen liked the look of his fine green velvet suit. Everyone liked the fact that the princess had become a very much nicer person. Before long it seemed sensible for the princess and the handsome young man to get married. They had lots of children who were not at all spoilt and everyone lived happily ever after. The golden ball and the green velvet suit were put away in a very dark cupboard.

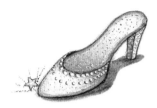

Cinderella

a retelling from the original tale by Charles Perrault

Once upon a time, when there were still fairy godmothers, there was a girl called Cinderella. She lived with her father and his new wife, and her two new step-sisters. The step-mother did not like Cinderella very much, mostly because she was so much nicer than her own two daughters. Cinderella was also much prettier. Oh, but the step-sisters were ugly!

Cinderella had to do all the work in the house as the ugly sisters were also very lazy. They spent all the father's money on new clothes and endless pairs of shoes, and then went off to parties leaving poor Cinderella with piles of stockings to mend.

One day a very grand invitation arrived. The prince was looking for a wife, and had decided to give a ball in three days time for all the young ladies in the land. The ugly sisters could talk about nothing else. They bought lots

of new dresses and many pairs
of matching shoes, and
then spent every hour
trying them all on. They
made Cinderella curl their
hair and iron their ribbons
and powder their noses.
Cinderella was so
exhausted running
around after them
that she had no time
to look into her own
wardrobe to choose
what she should wear.

In a waft of perfume,
the ugly sisters swept out
of the door into the carriage
without as much as a thank you to
Cinderella. She closed the door sadly, and went to sit by the
fire in the kitchen.

"I do wish I could have gone to the ball, too," she
sighed.

There was a sudden swirl of silver stars, and there in
front of Cinderella stood an old lady with a twinkle in her
eye, and a wand in her hand.

"You shall go to the ball, my dear Cinderella. I am
your fairy godmother," she said, smiling at Cinderella.

"Now, we must be quick, there is much to do! Please bring me a large pumpkin from the vegetable patch. Oh, and six mice from the barn, and you will find four lizards by the water butt."

Cinderella did as she was bid. With a wave of the wand,

the pumpkin was turned into a glittering golden coach and the mice into six pure white horses. The lizards became elegant footmen, dressed in green velvet.

"Now you, my dear," said the fairy godmother, turning to Cinderella. A wave of the wand, and Cinderella's old apron disappeared and there she stood in a white dress, glittering with golden stars. Her hair was piled on top of her head and it too was sprinkled with stars. On her feet were tiny glass slippers with diamonds sparkling in the heels.

"Enjoy yourself, my dear," said the fairy godmother, "but you must leave before midnight for then my magic ends and you will be back in your old apron with some mice and lizards at your feet!"

When Cinderella arrived at the ball everyone turned to look at this unknown beauty who had arrived so unexpectedly. The prince hurried over to ask her to dance and then would not dance with anyone else all evening. The ugly sisters were beside themselves with rage, which of course made them look even uglier.

Cinderella was enjoying herself so much that she forgot the fairy godmother's warning, so she had a terrible fright when the clock began to strike midnight. She turned from the prince with a cry and ran down the stairs of the palace into her carriage, and disappeared as suddenly as she had arrived. One of the tiny glass slippers with diamonds sparkling in the heels had slipped from her foot as she ran. The prince picked it up and turning to the crowded ballroom declared, "I shall marry the girl whose foot fits this slipper!"

Cinderella, meanwhile, had just managed to reach her garden gate when all her finery disappeared, and by the time the ugly sisters arrived home, both in a towering rage, she was sitting quietly by the fire.

The next morning, the prince went from house to house looking for the mystery girl whose foot would fit the tiny glass slipper. But no one had feet that small. He reached Cinderella's house where first one ugly sister and then the next tried to squash their huge feet into the slipper.

"Please let me try," said a quiet voice from the corner, and Cinderella stepped forward. The sisters just laughed in scorn but they soon stopped when they saw that the tiny slipper fitted Cinderella perfectly. There was a sudden swirl of silver stars, and there in front of Cinderella stood her fairy godmother with a twinkle in her eye, and a wand in her hand. In an instant, Cinderella was clothed in a gorgeous dress of cornflower blue silk decorated with pearls. On her feet she wore tiny white boots with blue tassels.

The prince whisked Cinderella off to the palace to meet the king and queen, and the wedding took place the very next day. Cinderella forgave the two ugly sisters, she was that sort of girl. But the prince insisted the sisters spent one day a week working in the palace kitchens just to remind them how horrid they had been to Cinderella.

Snow White and Rose Red

a retelling from the original story by the Brothers Grimm

Once upon a time there was a widow who had two daughters, Snow White and Rose Red. Snow White was quiet and gentle, Rose Red was wild as the hills, but they loved each other, and their mother, so the little house in the woods was a happy one.

One winter's evening as they all sat round the fire there was a knock at the door. Rose Red opened it and gave a scream. There stood a great big brown bear! But in a deep rumbly voice the bear said,

"Please do not be afraid. All I ask is that you let me sleep by your fire tonight. It is so cold outside."

"Of course you may shelter with us," said the mother. And she called the girls to set the soup on the stove and to put another log on the fire.

"Would you brush the snow from my fur, please?" asked the bear. Rose Red fetched the big broom and carefully

brushed the bear's great shaggy coat. Snow White gave him
a great bowl of hot soup and the bear gulped it down in
one. Then he stretched out in front of the fire and was soon
fast asleep.

In the morning Snow White let him out of the cottage
and he padded off into the forest through the deep snow.
But in the evening, he returned and once again Snow
White and Rose Red and their mother looked after him.
After that the bear came every night all through the winter,
and they all grew very fond of him. But when spring came,
the bear told them he would not be returning any more.

"I have to guard my treasure. Once the snows have

melted all kinds of wicked people try to steal it," he said and giving them all a hug he set off through the forest. Just as he passed through the garden gate, his fur caught on a nail. For a fleeting moment Snow White thought she saw a glint of gold, but the bear hurried off and was soon out of sight.

A few days later, Rose Red and Snow White were out gathering berries to make jam when they came alongside a fallen tree. Then they saw a very cross dwarf, tugging at his beard which was trapped by the great tree trunk.

"Well, don't stand there like a pair of silly geese! Come and help me!" he shrieked.

Well, no matter how hard they tugged Rose Red and Snow White were not strong enough to lift the tree, so Rose Red took her scissors out and snipped off the end of the dwarf's beard. He was absolutely furious, and snatched up a big bag of gold from the tree roots and disappeared without a word of thanks.

Some days later the girls' mother said she really fancied a piece of fish for supper, so they went down to the river to see what they could catch. But instead of a fish, there on the bank they found their friend the cross dwarf again. This time his beard was all caught up in his fishing line.

"Don't just stand there gawping," he yelled, "help me get free!"

Snow White tried to untangle it but it was impossible so she too snipped a piece off his beard. He was quite white with rage, but just grasped a casket of jewels that lay at the water's edge and turned away without a word of thanks.

It was the Spring Fair a few days later. The girls decided to go and buy some new ribbons for their hats, and their mother wanted needles for her embroidery, so they set off early in the morning. They had not gone far when they heard a terrible shrieking and crying. They ran towards the sound, and there once more was the cross dwarf, this time struggling in the huge talons of an eagle. They tugged and tugged and the eagle had to let go.

"You have torn my coat," muttered the ungrateful dwarf and picked up a basket of pearls and hobbled off as fast as possible. The girls just laughed and continued on their way to the fair.

They had a wonderful time, and it was quite late when they walked slowly home. The sun was just sinking behind a big rock when, to their astonishment, they came across the dwarf again. There spread out on the ground in front of him was a great pile of gold and precious jewels and pearls.

Suddenly the dwarf saw Snow White and Rose Red.

"Go away! Go away! You horrid girls are always in my way," he shouted. But just then there was a huge growl and the great brown bear stood by their side. With one huge paw he swiped the dwarf up, up into the sky and no one ever saw where he fell to

earth again. The bear turned towards
Snow White and Rose Red and as they
looked, his great shaggy coat fell away.
There stood a handsome young man, dressed
in a golden suit of the richest velvet.

"Do not be afraid, Snow White and Rose
Red," he said smiling. "Now you can see who I really
am. That wicked dwarf put a spell on me so he could steal
all my treasure, but you have broken the spell by
your kindness."

They all went home, laden with the treasure. They
talked long into the night, and it was all still true the next

morning! Snow White
married the handsome
young man who, by
great good fortune,
had a younger
brother who
married Rose
Red, so they all
lived happily
ever after.

But if you
ever find a dwarf
with half his beard
missing, I would be very
careful if I were you.

Rumpelstiltskin

a retelling from the original tale by the Brothers Grimm

nce upon a time there was a miller. He was a foolish man who was always boasting. Then he went too far.

The king was riding past the mill with his huntsmen one day. The miller's daughter was sitting in the doorway, spinning. The king could not help noticing that she was a very pretty girl so he began talking to her. Her father came bustling up and began to tell the king what a splendid daughter she was.

"Why, your Majesty, she can even spin straw into gold!" boasted the ridiculous miller.

Needless to say, the poor girl could do nothing of the sort but the king thought this was an excellent way to refill the palace treasure house which was rather empty, so he took her back to the palace. He put her in a room with a great pile of straw and told her he wanted to see it all spun into gold the next morning, or else it would be the worse for her.

As soon as the door was locked she began to cry. The task was impossible. Then she heard a thin little voice.

"Do stop crying! You will make the straw all wet, and then we will have no chance of turning it into gold!"

There in front of her stood a strange little man. He had a tiny round body with long skinny legs and huge feet. His clothes looked as if they had seen better days, and on his head he wore a tall battered-looking hat.

"If you give me your necklace, I will do what the king has asked of you," he snapped.

The miller's daughter

unclasped her necklace and handed it to the little man. He hid it deep in one of his pockets, and sat down by the spinning wheel. The spinning wheel turned in a blur. The pile of straw grew smaller, and the mound of shining gold grew higher. As the first light of day shone in through the window it was all done. The strange little man disappeared as suddenly as he had appeared.

The king was delighted with the great pile of gold, and asked the miller's daughter to marry him. She was too shy to reply so the king just took her silence as her agreement and married her anyway that afternoon.

For a while all was well. But then the treasure house grew empty again so once more the poor girl, now the queen, was locked in a room with a pile of straw and a spinning wheel.

As the queen wept, once more the strange little man appeared. The queen asked him to help her again, and offered him all the rich jewels she was wearing. But the strange little man was not interested in jewels this time.

"You must promise to give me your first born child," he whispered.

The queen was desperate. But she promised and the little man sat down at the spinning wheel. A great pile of gold appeared by the side of the spinning wheel, and by dawn the straw had all gone. The king was delighted and for a while all was well. Then the queen gave birth to a beautiful baby, and she remembered with dread her promise to the strange little man. Seven days after the baby was born, he appeared by the side of the cradle. The queen wept and wept.

"There you go again," said the little man crossly. "always crying!"

"I will do anything but let you have my baby," cried the queen.

"Very well then, anything to make you stop crying." said the little man, who by now was dripping wet from all the queen's tears. "If you can guess my name in three days, I will let you keep your baby," he said and disappeared as suddenly as he had appeared.

The next morning the little man appeared by the side of the cradle. The queen had sent messengers out far and wide to see if anyone knew the strange little man's name.

"Is it Lacelegs?" she asked.

"No!"

"Is it Wimbleshanks?"

"No!"

"Is it Bandyknees?"

"No!"

and the little man disappeared as suddenly as he had appeared.

The queen sent out even more messengers to the lands far beyond the borders of the kingdom. The second morning the strange little man appeared by the side of the cradle.

"Is it Bluenose?" the queen asked.

"No!"

"Is it Longtooth?"

"No!"

"Is it Skinnyribs?"

"No!" and the little man disappeared with a nasty laugh.

The queen waited up all night as her messengers came in one by one, and just as she was giving up all hope of saving her precious baby, in came the very last one. He was utterly exhausted but he brought the queen the best of news. In a deep, deep, dark forest he had found a strange little man dancing round a fire, singing this song.

Today I brew, today I bake,
Tomorrow I will the baby take.
The queen will lose the game,
Rumpelstiltskin is my name!

The strange little man appeared by the cradle. The queen pretended she still did not know his name.

"Is it Gingerteeth?" she asked.

"No!" said the little man, and he picked the baby up.

"Is it Silverhair?" asked the queen.

"No!" said the little man, and he started to walk towards the door, with a wicked smile.

"Is it Rumpelstiltskin?" asked the queen, and she ran up to the strange little man.

"Some witch told you that!" shrieked the little man, and he stamped his foot so hard that he fell through the floor and was never seen again. The queen told the king the whole story and he was so pleased his baby and his queen were safe that he forgot to be cross with the miller who had told such a terrible fib in the first place!

The Elves and the Shoemaker

a retelling from the original story by the Brothers Grimm

There was a time when everyone believed in elves. The shoemaker and his wife in this story certainly did!

The shoemaker worked very hard indeed from morn to night. The shoes he made were of the finest leather, and he was good with his hands, but business was slow. One night he found he only had enough leather left for one more pair of shoes. With a heavy heart, he cut the leather carefully and left the pieces ready on his work bench to sew the next morning. He blew out the candle, and crossed the yard from his little shop into the house.

"Wife, I do not know what we shall do. I have just cut out the very last piece of leather in the shop," he said sadly.

"Don't be too gloomy, husband," said his wife with a tired smile. "Perhaps you will be able to sell this last pair of shoes for a fine price. Wait and see what tomorrow brings!"

The next day the shoemaker was up early as usual. When he pulled back the shutters in the shop, you can imagine his surprise when he saw not pieces of leather ready to sew on the bench, but a fine pair of ladies' shoes with delicate pointed toes. The stitching was so fine you would think it had been done by mice. He put the shoes in the window of the shop, and before long a rich merchant came in and bought the shoes for his new wife, paying the poor shoemaker double the usual price. The shoemaker was delighted at this turn in his fortunes, and bought enough leather to make two new pairs of shoes.

Once again, he cut the leather carefully, and left the pieces ready on his work bench to sew the next morning

The next day the shoemaker was up even earlier than usual. His wife came with him as he went into the shop, and pulled back the shutters.

"Oh husband," she gasped, for there on the bench stood two pairs of the finest shoes she had ever seen. There was a green pair with red heels, and a pair so shiny and black the shoemaker could see his face in them. He put the shoes in the window, and very quickly in came a poet who bought the green pair with red heels, and not far behind him there was a parson who bought the shiny black pair. And both paid him a great deal of money for the splendid shoes with stitching so fine you would think it had been done by mice.

This continued for many days. The shoemaker would buy new leather and leave the pieces cut ready on his bench at night, and when he came back in the morning there would be the most exquisite shoes. The shoemaker's reputation spread, and his shop was soon full of customers, anxious to buy his special shoes. Before long the shoemaker and his wife were no longer poor, but they still lived simply as they had little wish for the luxuries of life. It was enough to be happy and healthy. One day, the wife said, "Husband, I think we must see who it is who has given us this great good fortune so we may thank them."

The shoemaker agreed, so that night after laying out the cut leather pieces and blowing out the candle, he and his wife hid behind the door of the shop. As the town hall clock struck midnight, they heard a scampering of tiny feet and little voices, laughing. Two tiny elves slid out from behind the skirting board and climbed up onto the bench where they were soon hard at work, stitching away with tiny stitches that were so fine they might have been done by mice. The elves sang as they stitched, sitting cross-legged on the bench. But 'oh!' they looked poor. Their trousers were ragged, their shirts were threadbare and their poor feet looked frozen as they had neither socks nor shoes. In a twinkling of an eye all the leather was used up, and there on the bench stood many pairs of shoes. The elves slipped away, laughing as they went.

The shoemaker and his wife looked at each other, and then and there both decided to reward the little craftsmen. The next day, the shoemaker took some scraps of green and yellow leather and, with the tiniest stitches possible, he made two little pairs of boots, yellow with green heels. The wife took her sewing basket and some scraps of cloth and, with the tiniest stitches possible, made two little pairs of red velvet trousers and two smart green jackets with shiny silver buttons. Then she knitted two little pairs of yellow socks, with the tiniest stitches possible.

That night, the shoemaker did not cut out any leather. Instead he laid out the clothes and the boots with the socks, and once again he and his wife hid behind the door of the shop.

As the town hall clock struck midnight, they heard a scampering of tiny feet and little voices, laughing. The two tiny elves slid out

from behind the skirting board and climbed up onto the bench. When they saw the gifts, they clapped their hands in delight and, laughing merrily, flung off their old rags and tried on their new clothes and the boots. They looked splendid. Still laughing and smiling, they slipped away behind the skirting board, and the shoemaker and his wife never saw them ever again.

But once a year when the shoemaker opened the shop in the morning, on his bench he would find a special pair of shoes with stitching so fine you would think it had been done by mice.

The Princess and the Pea

a retelling from the original story by Hans Christian Andersen

The prince was very fed up. Everyone in the court, from his father, the king, down to the smallest page, seemed to think it was time he was married. Now the prince would have been very happy to get married, but he did insist that his bride be a princess, a real true and proper princess. He had travelled the land and met plenty of nice girls who said they were princesses, but none, it seemed to him, were really true and proper princesses. Either their manners were not quite exquisite enough, or their feet were much too big. So he sat in the palace, reading dusty old history books and getting very glum.

One night, there was the most terrible storm. Rain was lashing down, and thunder and lightning rolled and flashed round the palace. The wind kept blowing out the candles, and everyone huddled closer to the fire. Suddenly there was a great peal from the huge front door bell.

And there, absolutely dripping wet, stood a princess. Well, she said she was a princess, but never did anyone look less like a princess. Her hair was plastered to her head, her dress was wringing wet and her silk shoes were covered in mud. She was quite alone, without even the smallest maid, and just where had she come from? But she kept insisting she was a princess.

We will see about that, thought the queen. While the dripping girl sat sipping a mug of warm milk and honey, the queen went to supervise the making of the bed in the second-best spare bedroom. She didn't think it necessary to put their late night visitor in the best spare bedroom, after all she might only be a common-or-garden duchess. The queen told the maids to take all the bedclothes and the mattress off the bed. Then she placed one single pea right on the middle of the bedstead. Next the maids piled twenty mattresses on top of the pea, and then twenty feather quilts on top of the mattresses. And thus the girl was left for the night.

In the morning, the queen swept into the bedroom in her dressing gown and asked the girl how she had slept.

"I didn't sleep a wink all night." said the girl. "There was a great, hard lump in the middle of the bed. It was quite dreadful. I am sure I am black and blue all over!"

Now everyone knew she really must be a princess, for only a real princess could be as soft-skinned as that. The prince was delighted, and insisted they got married at once, and they lived very happily ever after. They always slept in very soft beds, and the pea was placed in the museum, where it probably still is today.

The Three Wishes

an English folk tale

There was once a poor fisherman who lived by the edge of the sea in a tumbledown old cottage. He lived with his wife, who was always grumbling no matter how hard the fisherman worked.

One evening he threw the nets out for one last try before it grew dark. He had caught nothing all day. As he began pulling the nets in the fisherman's hopes rose: the nets were heavy. But when he hauled them over the side of the boat there was only one tiny fish lying at the bottom. Then the fish spoke. The fisherman rubbed his eyes in astonishment.

"Please throw me back into the sea," said the fish. "I am so small I would not make much of a meal for you."

But the fisherman was tired and hungry.

"Even though you are small I cannot throw you back. My wife would not be pleased if I came home empty handed." he said with a deep sigh.

"I will grant you the first three wishes made in your cottage if you let me go," said the fish, "but I should warn you that wishes do not always give you what you really want."

Well, the fisherman did not hear the fish's warning. All he heard was the bit about three wishes, and he thought that finally his grumbling wife could have whatever she wanted. So he carefully untangled the tiny fish from the nets and placed it back in the sea. With a flick of its tail the fish disappeared deep, deep under water.

The fisherman ran all the way home and in great excitement told her all about the tiny fish. But instead of being pleased, she just shouted at him as usual.

"Trust you to believe such a thing! Whoever heard of a talking fish, you must be daft husband," and she slammed down a plate of dry bread and a rind of cheese in front of the poor fisherman.

"I wish this was a plate of fine sausages, I am so hungry," said the fisherman wistfully.

No sooner were the words out of his mouth than there was a wonderful smell and there in front of him was a plate of sizzling sausages! He was delighted and reached for his knife when his wife yelled at him,

"Why couldn't you have wished for something better? We could have had chests of gold and fine clothes to wear!" and this from the woman who had refused to believe his story only a few moments before. "You stupid fool! I wish the sausages were at the end of your nose!"

There was a ghastly silence as the wife looked at her poor husband. Hanging from the end of his nose was a great string of sausages. The fisherman remembered what the fish had said – the first three wishes made in the cottage.

The fisherman and his wife pulled and pulled at the sausages, but it was no good. They were stuck fast. There was nothing for it, they would have to use the last wish.

"I wish the sausages would disappear," said the fisherman sadly, and they did in a flash. So there they sat, the poor fisherman and his grumbling wife. No delicious supper of sizzling sausages and, much worse, no magic wishes. The fisherman never caught the tiny fish again, and as far as I know, his wife never stopped grumbling. Wishes do not always give you what you really want.

Animals Big and Small

The Lion and the Mouse

a retelling from Aesop's Fables

The lion was very hungry. As he padded through the tall grass, something rustled by his feet. He reached out a great paw, and there was a squeak. He had caught a tiny mouse by the tail.

"Oh please let me go, dear lion," cried the tiny mouse. "I should be no more than a single mouthful for you. And I promise I will be able to help you some day."

The lion roared with laughter. The thought of a tiny mouse being able to help such a huge creature as himself amused him so much that he did let the mouse go.

"He would not have made much of a meal anyway," smiled the lion.

The mouse scuttled away, calling out to the lion,

"I shall not forget my promise!"

Many days and nights later the lion was padding through the tall grass again when he suddenly fell into a deep pit. A net was flung over him, and he lay there helpless, caught by some hunters. He twisted and turned but he could not free himself. The hunters just laughed at his struggles and went off to fetch a cart to carry the great lion back to their village.

As he lay there, the lion heard a tiny voice in his ear.

"I promised you I would be able to help you one day."

It was the tiny mouse! And straight away he began to gnaw through the rope that held the lion fast. He gnawed and chewed, and chewed and gnawed, and eventually he chewed and gnawed right through the rope and the lion was free. With a great bound, he leapt out of the pit and then reached back, very gently, to lift the tiny mouse out too.

"I shall never forget you, mouse. Thank you for remembering your promise and saving me," purred the great lion.

So the tiny mouse was able to help the great lion. One good turn deserves another, you see?

Why the Manx Cat has no Tail

a myth from the Isle of Man

The rain was falling in torrents, and there were great storm clouds building up. The rivers were overflowing and the fields looked like lakes. Noah decided that the time had come to fill his ark as planned with two of every animal that lived. He called his sons Shem and Ham and Japeth and they began rounding up the animals and leading them gently onto the ark.

First came the big beasts, the giraffes and lions and elephants. Then came the cows and the sheep and the pigs. Then came the foxes and the rabbits, but not together of course. Then came the birds and the grasshoppers and the ants, who were rather nervous of the elephants' feet. Finally came the dogs, but only one cat, a big ginger tom cat. The she-cat, who was a stripy tabby, had decided that she would like to go mousing one last time, as she realised she would not be able to eat a fellow passenger when they were all cooped up in the ark.

Mrs Noah called and called her, but still she did not come. Cats are always contrary and she was no exception. Noah looked at the rising water and told Mrs Noah that he would have to pull up the gangplank as the ark would soon be afloat. All the other animals were settling in to their various stalls, and what a noise there was! Roaring and mooing, trumpeting and baaing, snorting and squawking. Toes and flippers and trotters and paws got stood on, fur and feathers were ruffled and horns and long tails got stuck, but eventually everyone was in place.

Noah began to pull the great door of the ark to, and just as he was about to shut it fast, up pranced the she-cat, soaking wet but licking her lips. She managed to slip through the gap in the nick of time but her great plume of a tail was caught in the door as it slammed shut. She turned round and her entire tail was cut off! The cat was very

cross, but Noah told her it was entirely her own fault and she would have to wait until they found land again before she could have her tail mended.

Forty days and forty nights later, the flood was over and Noah opened the great door of the ark once more. First out was the she-cat, and she ran and ran until she found the Isle of Man, and there she stopped, too ashamed for anyone else to see her. Ever since then the cats from the Isle of Man have had no tails. Nowadays they are rather proud to be different.

Chicken Licken

an English folk tale

One fine day Chicken Licken went for a walk in the woods. Now Chicken Licken was not very bright, and he was also rather inclined to act first and think after. So when an acorn fell on his head, he decided immediately that the sky must be falling in. He set off as fast as he could to tell the king. On the way he met Henny Penny and Cocky Locky.

"I am off to tell the king that the sky is falling in," he clucked importantly.

"We will come too," said Henny Penny and Cocky Locky.

So Chicken Licken, Henny Penny and Cocky Locky set off to find the King. On the way they met Ducky Lucky and Drakey Lakey.

"We are off to tell the king that the sky is falling in," clucked Chicken Licken importantly.

66

"We will come too," said Ducky Lucky and Drakey Lakey.

So Chicken Licken, Henny Penny, Cocky Locky, Ducky Lucky and Drakey Lakey all set off to find the king. On the way they met Goosey Loosey and Turkey Lurkey.

"We are off to tell the king that the sky is falling in," clucked Chicken Licken importantly.

"We will come too," said Goosey Loosey and Turkey Lurkey.

So Chicken Licken, Henny Penny, Cocky Locky, Ducky Lucky, Drakey Lakey, Goosey Loosey and Turkey Lurkey all set off to find the king. On the way they met Foxy Loxy.

"We are off to tell the king that the sky is falling in," clucked Chicken Licken importantly.

"What a good thing I met you all," said Foxy Loxy with a cunning smile. "I know the way, follow me."

So Chicken Licken, Henny Penny, Cocky Locky, Ducky Lucky, Drakey Lakey, Goosey Loosey and Turkey Lurkey all set off behind Foxy Loxy. He led them all straight to his den where he ate every single one of them for his dinner! So the king never heard that the sky was falling in. (It didn't, of course.)

The Three Little Pigs

an English folk tale

There once was a mother pig who had three little pigs. They were very poor indeed, and the day came when the mother pig could no longer look after the family. She sent the three little pigs out into the wide world to seek their fortunes.

The first little pig met a man carrying a big bundle of straw.

"Oh, please may I have that bundle of straw to build myself a house?" asked the first little pig. The man was tired of carrying the bundle of straw so he gladly gave it to the first little pig.

The first little pig built a very fine house out of the bundle of straw, and he lived there very happily. Then along came a big bad wolf.

"Little pig, little pig, let me come in!" shouted the wolf.

"No, no, not by the hair on my chinny chin chin. I'll not let you in," squeaked the first little pig.

"Then I'll huff and I'll puff, and I'll blow your house down," yelled the wolf. And he did. He huffed and he puffed and he blew the straw house down. The first little pig ran away as fast as his trotters would carry him.

Now the second little pig met a man carrying a bundle of sticks.

"Oh, please may I have that bundle of sticks to build myself a house?" asked the second little pig. The man was tired of carrying the bundle of sticks so he gladly gave it to the second little pig.

The second little pig built a very fine house out of the bundle of sticks, and he lived there very happily. Then along came the big bad wolf.

"Little pig, little pig, let me come in!" shouted the wolf.

"No, no, not by the hair on my chinny chin chin. I'll not let you in," squeaked the second little pig.

"Then I'll huff and I'll puff, and I'll blow your house down," yelled the wolf. And he did. He huffed and he puffed and he blew the stick house down. The second little pig ran away as fast as his trotters would carry him.

Now the third little pig met a man carrying a big load of bricks.

"Oh, please may I have that load of bricks to build myself a house?" asked the third little pig. The man was very tired indeed from carrying the big load of bricks so he gladly gave it to the third little pig.

The third little pig built a very fine house out of the big load of bricks, and he lived there very happily. Then along came the big bad wolf.

"Little pig, little pig, let me come in!" shouted the wolf.

"No, no, not by the hair on my chinny chin chin. I'll not let you in," squeaked the third little pig.

"Then I'll huff and I'll puff, and I'll blow your house down," yelled the wolf. And he tried. He huffed and he puffed but he could not blow the brick house down.

"Little pig, little pig, I am coming down your chimney to get you," bellowed the wolf.

"Please yourself," called the third little pig who was busy with some preparations of his own.

"Little pig, little pig, I have my front paws down your chimney," threatened the wolf.

"Please yourself," called the third little pig who was still

busy with some
preparations of his own.

"Little pig, little pig,
I have my great
bushy tail down your
chimney," called
the wolf.

"Please yourself,"
called the third little
pig who was now
sitting in his rocking
chair by the fireside.

"Little pig, little
pig, here I come!"
and with a great rush
and a huge SPLOSH!
the big bad wolf fell
right into the big pot
of boiling water that
the clever little pig had

placed on the fire, right under the
chimney. The wolf scrabbled and splashed and scrambled
out of the big pot and ran as fast as ever he could right out
of the front door. And he was never seen again. The third
little pig managed to find his two brothers, and they went
and fetched their mother. And they are all still living
happily together in the little brick house.

Billy The Kid Goes Wild

by Francesca Simon

Billy the Kid had big plans. When he had finished munching the blankets he was going to gobble some tasty paper bags he'd seen blowing about in Silver Meadow. Then he wanted to visit Muddy Pond, watch the fish, and nibble some thorny bushes. Then he was off to Gabby Goose's birthday party. So you can imagine how Billy felt when his father interrupted.

"Nap time," said Father Goat.

"Oh no," said Billy.

"Oh yes," said his father. "If you don't have a nap you'll be too tired for Gabby's party."

"No, I won't," said Billy.

"Yes, you will," said Father Goat.

"But I'm not tired," said Billy.

Trot poked his head over the stable door.

"I'll help Billy feel sleepy," said Trot.

"Come on Billy, I'll race you across Butterfly Field."

Off they galloped.

"I won," shouted Billy the Kid. "Race you back."

So Trot and Billy zoomed back to the stable.

"Again!" shouted Billy. Back and forth, back and forth they ran. At last Trot stood panting.

"Let's race to Far Away Field," said Billy.

"If you don't mind, Billy, I think I'll just rest for a moment," said Trot, yawning. He closed his eyes and fell asleep.

"Nap time," said Father Goat.

"But I'm not tired," said Billy the Kid.

"You're going to be too tired for Gabby's party," said Father Goat.

"No, I'm not," said Billy.

Squeaky the cat scampered over.

"I'll help Billy feel sleepy," said Squeaky. "Come on

Billy, let's do somersaults all the way to Muddy Pond. Last one there is a ninny."

Off they somersaulted.

"I won," shouted Billy. "Let's race again."

Head over heels they rolled. At last Squeaky stood panting.

"Let's hop backwards to the haystack now," said Billy.

"If you don't mind, Billy," said Squeaky, yawning, "I think I'll just lie down for a moment."

She closed her eyes and fell asleep.

"Nap time," said Father Goat.

"But I'm still not tired," said Billy.

Buster the dog and Rosie the calf strolled by.

"We'll help Billy feel sleepy," said Buster. "Come on Billy, let's see who can bellow the loudest."

"RUFF RUFF RUFF"

"MOOOOOOOOOOOOOOOOOOoo"

"MAAAAAAAAAAAAAAAAAAAAAAAAAA!"

"RUFF RUFF RUFF"

"MOOOOOOOOOOOOooo"

"MAAAAAAAAAAAAAAAAAAAAAA"

"RUFF RUFF RUFF"

"MOOOOOOOOOOOOoo"

"MAAAAAAAAAAAAAAAAAAAAA!"

Back and forth across the farmyard they hullabalooed, louder and louder, barking, mooing and bleating. At last Buster and Rosie stood panting.

"That was fantastic," said Billy the Kid.

"Let's go and play with Tam and Tilly now."

"If you don't mind, Billy, I'll just lie down for a moment," said Buster, yawning.

"Me too," said Rosie. They closed their eyes and fell asleep.

Just then Gabby ran out of her shed, honking.

"Party time!" she yelled.

"Wake up, Trot! Wake up, Squeaky! Wake up, Buster! Wake up, Rosie!" shouted Billy. "It's party time."

Everyone had a lovely time at Gabby's party. They played musical statues, pass the parcel, and pin the hat on the farmer. Then everyone ate lots and lots of hay and corn and oats.

Well, almost everyone.

Why the Robin has a Red Breast

an Inuit legend

In the land where it is always winter all the time, there once lived a man and his son. It was so cold that they lived in a house made of snow, and their clothes were all made of fur.

But even with the warm furs it was cold in the snow house. The man and his son needed a fire as well. They needed it to heat the snow house. They needed it to have hot food to eat. So they could never let their fire go out as without it they would surely die.

Whenever the father went out hunting, he would leave his son with a great pile of wood. The fire burned brightly by the entrance to the snow house. The first thing the boy had learned was never ever to let the fire go out.

Now one of the creatures the man was always hunting was the great white bear. The great white bear hated the man and used all his cunning to hide from the hunter. The bear saw that the fire was precious to the man and his son. He thought that if only he could stamp out the fire with his huge white paws, the man and his son would fall into such a deep cold sleep that they would never wake again. So the great white bear watched and waited for his chance.

One day the father fell ill. All day he tossed and turned on his bed. He was not able to go out hunting. The great white bear watched as the son fed the fire with sticks as his father had taught him. The next day, the father was no better. The son looked after him as well as he could but by now he was growing hungry. At night he could hear the great white bear prowling round the snow house, and he was afraid. The third day the father hardly moved at all, and the boy had to fight to keep his eyes open. He put some more sticks onto the fire, but eventually he could keep his eyes open no longer. He fell into a deep, deep sleep.

The great white bear pounced. He stomped and stamped and put the fire out with his huge white paws. Then he padded away, leaving the boy and his father to their fate. It grew bitterly cold in the snow house. Frost and snow gathered round the furs on the bed, and round the boy's furry hood. Still he slept on and on. Both father and

son grew stiff with cold.

The boy had one special friend. It was a tiny little brown bird called a robin. The boy used to feed the robin and let it shelter in the snow house when the blizzards blew. The little bird came hopping up to the snow house and he saw right away that all was not well. He twittered round the boy's head, calling to warn him that the fire had gone out. But still the boy slept on, exhausted by all his efforts to look after his father. The robin scratched among the ashes where the great white bear had stomped, desperately looking for just one tiny ember that was still alight. He found one tiny spark, and he began fanning it with his little wings. He flapped his wings for all he was worth and slowly, slowly the flame caught. It spread to another piece of stick, and still the robin flapped and flapped his wings.

The heat was growing now, and the robin's feathers were scorching. More and more sticks caught alight, and the brave little robin felt his chest feathers burn red with heat.

The boy woke with a start and leapt to his feet. He saw the fire was nearly out, and he rushed to pile on more sticks. He did not see his tiny friend flutter off into the darkness outside. It grew warmer in the snow house, and to his great joy the boy saw his father was stirring on the bed. His eyes were clear and the sickness had passed. In the distance, the great white bear stumped off a long way from the snow house. He could see he was not going to get the better of the hunter and his son.

The next time the robin came to the snow house for food, the boy was puzzled to see the little brown bird now had a bright red breast. But he was never to know why.

Androcles and the Lion

a retelling from the Fables of Phaedrus

Many thousands of years ago there lived a poor slave called Androcles. Life was very miserable for slaves. They barely had enough to eat, and if they didn't work hard enough they were sent to Rome to be thrown to the lions.

One day, Androcles had a chance to escape. He didn't hesitate. He ran and ran, and ran again until he was utterly exhausted, so he crawled into a forest to hide until he regained his strength. He was just settling down to try to sleep when a great lion hobbled out from behind a tree. At first, Androcles was absolutely petrified. He was just thinking how very unfair life was that he should manage to escape, only to be eaten by a lion, when he realised the lion was not about to jump on him, but was holding out his paw helplessly. Androcles stepped cautiously towards the lion. The paw was all swollen and bleeding, and when Androcles looked closely he could see why. There was a huge thorn stuck in between the claws, which must have been causing the lion considerable pain.

Androcles pulled the thorn out, and cleaned the wound before wrapping it in leaves to keep it dry. The great lion licked Androcles with his very rough tongue and then lay down beside him and went to sleep. He kept Androcles warm all night. In the morning the lion slipped away very early and Androcles continued on his way.

Years passed. But one day Androcles' luck ran out and he was captured by his master's men and sent into the arena to fight. The trap door was opened and a huge lion came

bounding up to Androcles. He closed his eyes, waiting for certain death. But then he felt a rough tongue licking his face. It was his lion! The crowds cheered with delight at this unexpected turn of events, and the emperor made Androcles tell the story of how he had taken the thorn out of the lion's paw. The emperor decided to free Androcles, and said that the lion could go with him. Androcles kept the lion's coat well brushed and his paws free of thorns, while the lion kept Androcles warm in bed at night, and so they both lived to a very ripe old age together.

The Ugly Duckling

a retelling from the original story by Hans Christian Andersen

The mother duck was waiting for her eggs to hatch. Slowly the first shell cracked and first a tiny bill and then a little yellow wing appeared. Then with a great rush, a bedraggled yellow duckling fell out. He stretched his wings and began to clean his feathers. Soon he stood proudly beside his mother, watching as his sisters and brothers all pushed their way out of their shells.

There was only one shell left. It was the largest, and the mother duck wondered why it was taking so much longer than the others. She wanted to take her babies down to the river for their first swimming lesson. There was a sudden loud crack, and there lay quite the biggest and ugliest duckling she had ever seen. He wasn't even yellow. His feathers were dull brown and grey.

"Oh dear," said the mother duck.

She led the family down to the river, the ugly duckling trailing along behind the others. They all splashed into the water, and were soon swimming gracefully, all except the ugly duckling who looked large and ungainly even on the water.

"Oh dear," said the mother duck.

The whole family set off for the farmyard where they were greeted with hoots and moos and barks and snorts from all the other animals.

"Whatever is that?" said the rooster, pointing rudely at the ugly duckling. All the other ducklings huddled round their mother and tried to pretend the ugly duckling was not with them.

"Oh dear," said the mother duck.

The ugly duckling felt very sad and lonely. No one seemed to like him, so he ran away from the farmyard and

hid in some dark reeds by the
river. Some hunters came
by with their loud noisy
guns and big fierce dogs.
The ugly duckling
paddled deeper
into the reeds,
trembling with
fear. Only later
in the day, as it
was growing
dark, did the
ugly duckling
dare move from
his hiding place.

All summer he
wandered over fields and
down rivers. Everywhere he went people
laughed and jeered at him, and all the other ducks he met
just hissed at him or tried to bite his tail. As well as being
ugly, the duckling was very lonely and unhappy. Soon
winter came and the rivers began to freeze over. One day
the duckling found himself trapped in the ice. He tucked his
head under his wing, and decided that his short life must
have come to an end.

He was still there early the next morning when a
farmer came by on his way to feed the cows in the fields.

The farmer broke the ice with his shoe, and wrapped the ugly duckling in his jacket then carried him home to his children. They put the poor frozen ugly duckling in a box by the fire, and as he thawed out they fed him and stroked his feathers. And there the ugly duckling stayed through the winter, growing bigger all the time.

Now the farmer's wife had never had much time for the ugly duckling. He was always getting under her feet in the kitchen, and he was so clumsy that he kept knocking things over. He spilt the milk in the bucket from the cow. He put his great feet in the freshly churned butter. He was just a nuisance, and one day the farmer's wife had enough. So, in a rage, she chased him out of her kitchen, out of the farmyard and through the gate down the lane.

It was a perfect spring day. The apple trees were covered in blossom, the grass was green and the air was filled with the sound of birdsong. The ugly duckling wandered down to the river, and there he saw three magnificent pure white swans. They were beautiful and so graceful as they glided over towards the bank where he stood. He waited for them to hiss at him and beat the water with their great wings to frighten him away, but they didn't do any such thing. Instead they called him to come and join them. At first he thought it was a joke, but they asked him again.

He bent down to get into the water, and there looking back at him was his own reflection. But where was the ugly duckling? All he could see was another great and magnificent swan. He was a swan! Not an ugly duckling but a swan. He lifted his great long elegant neck, and called in sheer delight, "I am a swan! I am a SWAN!" and he sailed gracefully over the water to join his real family.

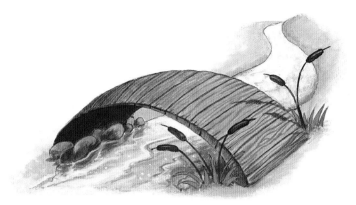

The Three Billy Goats Gruff

a folk tale from Europe

In a mountain valley beside a rushing river, there lived three billy goats. One was very small, one was middle-sized and one was huge, and they were called the Three Billy Goats Gruff. Every day they would eat the lush green grass beside the river, and they were very content.

One day, however, the Three Billy Goats Gruff decided they would like to cross the river and see if the grass was any greener on the other side. The grass was actually no greener, nor was it any tastier, but they all felt they would like a change. First they had to find a way to cross the rushing river. They trotted a good way upstream before they found a little wooden bridge. After a good supper of lush green grass, they decided to wait until the next morning before crossing the little wooden bridge, so they settled down for the night.

Now, what the Three Billy Goats Gruff did not know
was that under the little wooden bridge there lived a very
mean and grumpy troll. He could smell the Three Billy
Goats Gruff, and he thought they smelled very good to eat.
So the next morning when the Three Billy Goats Gruff had
had a good breakfast of lush green grass, the troll was
hiding under the little wooden bridge, waiting for his
chance to have a good breakfast too.

"That little wooden bridge does not look too strong,"
said the very small Billy Goat Gruff. "I will go across first to
see if it is safe," and he trotted across the little wooden
bridge. But when he was only halfway across, the mean
and grumpy troll leapt out of his hiding place.

"Who is that trit-trotting across my bridge?" he roared.
"I am going to eat you up!"

But the very small Billy Goat Gruff wasn't ready to be

eaten up just yet, so he bravely said to the mean and grumpy troll, "You don't want to eat a skinny, bony thing like me. Just wait till my brother comes across, he is much bigger," and with a skip and a hop, the very small Billy Goat Gruff ran across the bridge to the lush green grass on the other side.

The middle-sized Billy Goat Gruff started to cross the little wooden bridge, but when he was only halfway across, the mean and grumpy troll roared at him.

"Who is that trit-trotting across my bridge?" he roared. "I am going to eat you up!"

But the middle-sized Billy Goat Gruff wasn't ready to be eaten up just yet either, so he bravely said to the mean and grumpy troll,

"You don't want to eat a skinny, bony thing like me. Just wait till my brother comes across, he is even bigger," and with a skip and a hop, the middle-sized Billy Goat Gruff ran across the bridge to the lush green grass on the other side.

Now the huge Billy Goat Gruff had been watching all

the time. He smiled to himself and stepped out onto the little wooden bridge. By this time the mean and grumpy troll was getting very hungry indeed, and he was even meaner and grumpier when he was hungry. He didn't even bother to hide, but stood in the middle of the bridge looking at the huge Billy Goat Gruff who came trotting up to him.

"Who is that trit-trotting across my bridge?" he roared. "I am going to eat you up!"

"Oh no, you won't!" said the huge Billy Goat Gruff, and he lowered his head and with his huge horns he biffed the mean and grumpy troll into the rushing river. The water carried him far away down the river, and he was never seen again. The Three Billy Goats Gruff lived happily for many more years eating the lush green grass, and they were able to cross the rushing river just whenever they wanted!

The Amazing Talking Pig

by Mick Gowar

It was a cold autumn night on Brown's Farm. Mr Brown, the farmer, had finished washing up his supper things, and was just settling down in his comfy armchair to read his library book, when there was a gentle tap-tappity-tap on the front door.

"Bother!" muttered Mr Brown, grumpily. "I was just getting comfortable."

He looked at the clock on the mantelpiece: it was half-past nine.

"Who can that be, so late?" he wondered.

Cautiously, Mr Brown opened the door and looked out. There was no one there. He was just closing the door when he heard a cough. Mr Brown peered out into the darkened farmyard; there was still no one there. He started to close the door again.

"Ah-hem, ah-hem!" said a voice.

It seemed to be coming from the step. Mr Brown looked down and saw, to his astonishment, a small pink pig.

"Hullo," said the pig, politely.

"WAAAH!" yelled Mr Brown, staggering back.

"I said: hullo," repeated the pig.

"You… you… you… can…" spluttered Mr Brown.

"… come in?" suggested the pig. "Thanks very much. I will."

And it walked past Mr Brown and into the warm cosy sitting room.

"Wow!" exclaimed the pig, looking round the room. "This is some sty!" It sniffed the carpet. "And that is what I call High Class Straw!"

Mr Brown tottered unsteadily into the room.

"But… but… but…" he gasped, "you can… can…"

"… sit down and make myself at home?" suggested the pig. "Ta, very much!"

With a quick spring it jumped into Mr Brown's armchair.

"Very nice!" said the pig, snuggling down into the

cushions. "And what's this?"

It sniffed Mr Brown's library book, which he'd left open on the chair. "Oooh! I see I'm just in time for a snack," said the pig, licking its lips. "Goody!" And it tore out a page and began chewing.

"Not bad," said the pig thoughtfully, as it swallowed the page. "I prefer a little warm swill, myself, but if this is all you've got in the house to eat, who am I to complain?"

"You can…you can…talk!" Mr Brown finally managed to stammer out.

"Oh brilliant!" said the pig sarcastically. "Of course I can talk, what do you think I am, thick or something?"

"No, no, no," replied Mr Brown hastily. "It's just that…well …but … but you've never spoken to me before."

"Haven't needed to," explained the pig. "Everything was OK until now. Nice food, clean straw, cosy sty, good conversation with the other pigs. What more could a pig want? But tonight? Brrrr! That sty is not the place to spend a cold night, I can tell you. Talk about freezing? I was colder than a penguin's bottom! So I said to myself: Horatio – that's my name, by the way – Horatio, I said, this is the time of year when a pig needs a warm fire, a cup of hot cocoa, and a proper bed with plenty of warm blankets. So here I am."

Mr Brown shook his head in amazement.

The pig suddenly looked worried. "You do have cocoa, don't you?" it asked.

"Er…yes…" replied Mr Brown.

"Great!" said the pig. "I like two sugars. Oh, and don't let the milk boil. I can't stand skin on my cocoa."

Mr Brown walked out to the kitchen like a robot in shock. He opened the fridge and, as if in a dream, he poured a pint of milk into a saucepan and put it on the hotplate.

As he waited for the milk

to heat, Mr Brown tried to get used to the idea of his amazing guest.

Fantastic! he said to himself.

"Unbelievable! A talking pig! I've never heard of anything like it before. I'm sure it must be the only talking pig in the whole world."

"Yoo-hoo! Mr Brown!" called the pig from the sitting room. "Don't forget what I said: no skin on my cocoa, please."

Mr Brown poured the cocoa into two cups: one for him, one for the pig. Then he had second thoughts, and poured the pig's cocoa into a bigger cup. Then he had third thoughts, and poured a large whisky into his cocoa. (He'd had a nasty shock; he needed a little something.)

The only one in the whole world… thought Mr Brown, as the whisky glugged into his cup. *This could make me famous! I can see the headlines in all the papers: FARMER BROWN AND HIS AMAZING TALKING PIG! I'll be on radio and TV, too! That pig could make me rich! That pig could make me a millionaire. I'd better be very nice to that pig.*

"Here you are," said Mr Brown, putting the pig's cocoa down in front of the fire. "And if you want anything else, anything at all, just tell me…"

By midnight, Mr Brown bitterly regretted his promise to give the pig anything it wanted. There seemed to be nothing that the pig didn't want. Mr Brown had never had to work so hard in all his life.

First the pig had wanted a second cup of cocoa. Then the pig had asked for a snack.

"A proper one this time, please!"

So Mr Brown had made up a special warm mash to the pig's favourite recipe. The pig had sat in the armchair yelling out orders, while Mr Brown scurried frantically in the kitchen.

"Two jars of strawberry jam – large ones – and one tin of treacle. Now, crumble in sixteen Weetabix. Got that?"

"Er, yes…" Mr Brown had replied, desperately crumbling Weetabix as fast as he could.

"Now mix up four pounds of creamed potatoes, fresh, mind, none of that powdered rubbish, and use real butter. Humans may not be able to tell the difference between

margarine and butter, but pigs can! And when you've creamed the potatoes, add two jars of Marmite and three pounds of stewed prunes. And finally, two tablespoons of Double Strength Madras Curry Powder, for that extra tingle, know what I mean?"

After its meal, the pig demanded a bubble bath, in the old tin tub in front of the fire.

"I can't stand cold bathrooms," the pig had explained.

Poor Mr Brown. He'd had to run between the kitchen and the sitting room with pots and pans and kettles of hot water. Then he'd had to mix up a bubble bath using two giant containers of washing-up liquid and a bottle of very expensive after-shave his sister Lydia had given him for his birthday.

Mr Brown was now weak with tiredness. The pig wasn't.

"Let's have some music," said the pig. "I see you've got a banjo. Let's have a sing-song!"

So Mr Brown played the banjo until his fingertips were sore and throbbing, while the pig sang every song that Mr Brown knew in the most awful squealing tenor voice that

Mr Brown had ever heard. The pig also changed all the words so that all the songs were about pigs. Its favourite songs were: 'Old MacDonald Had A Pig' and 'All Pigs Bright And Beautiful'.

"I'm beginning to feel a little sleepy," said the pig, when it had finished singing.

Mr Brown breathed a huge sigh of relief.

"So, time for a bedtime story, or two!" announced the pig.

Bleary-eyed and sore-throated, Mr Brown stumbled through *The Three Little Pigs* and *The Three Billy Goats Gruff*, but with the goats changed to pigs, of course.

"Well," said the pig, eventually, "time for bed! I mustn't miss my beauty sleep. Where's my room?"

Mr Brown led the way upstairs, and into the guest bedroom.

"Oh, dear," said the pig, inspecting the bed. "Tut-tut! This is no good! The bed's too narrow, and the mattress is much too lumpy. I'll have to sleep in your bed."

Wearily, Mr Brown led the way to his own room.

"Not bad," said the pig, snuggling under the covers. "But still not perfect."

"What's the matter now?" groaned Mr Brown.

"No hotty-totty," replied the pig.

"No what?" asked Mr Brown.

"No hot-water bottle," said the pig. "You don't want me to catch cold, do you?"

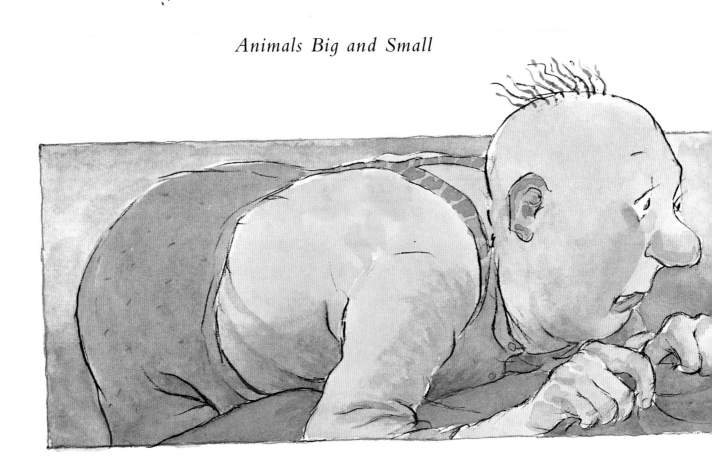

Mr Brown staggered downstairs to fetch the hot-water bottle.

"And I forgot, I'll need a drink of water, too," the pig said as Mr Brown came back into the room.

With a weary groan Mr Brown fetched a bowl of water.

"Now a good-night kiss …" said the pig, puckering its snout.

"Do I have to?" asked Mr Brown.

"Yes," said the pig, "you do!"

Mr Brown woke up. He was still in his armchair. The fire was out, and the morning light was glinting through a thin crack between his curtains. His library book had fallen face down on the floor at his feet. He looked at the clock on the mantelpiece: it was half-past seven.

The pig!

Mr Brown sat up, horrified. Then he chuckled to himself. It had all been a dream. He must have fallen asleep in his chair and dreamt the whole thing!

Mr Brown got to his feet and stretched. Then he bent down and began to rake out the cold ashes of his fire.

"WAAAAH!" yelled Mr Brown, as something wet and snout-like tapped him on the back of the neck.

"Good morning!" said the cheerful, snuffly voice behind him. "What's for breakfast? I'm ravenous!"

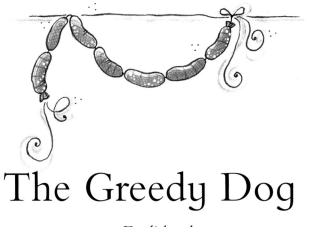

The Greedy Dog

an English tale

There was once a very greedy dog who just ate and ate. Whenever he saw anything that looked good enough to eat, he would just open his mouth and gobble it all up. The postman wouldn't come near the house anymore, ever since the greedy dog mistook his ankle for an early breakfast. He would stand at the gate and throw the letters in the general direction of the letterbox. The paperboy just refused to go anywhere near. Visitors knew they had to come with a juicy bone or they wouldn't get as far as the front door.

One day the greedy dog was out wandering round the shops. He loved doing this as there were always lots of really good smells for him to investigate, and sometimes old ladies, who didn't know any better, would give him sticky buns to eat.

As he walked past the butcher's shop, the greedy dog started to lick his lips. There in the window was a great big steak. It looked juicy and very good to eat. The greedy dog decided that the steak would make a very nice meal. So he watched and waited outside the shop. Soon one of his favourite old ladies walked down the street and into the butcher's shop. The greedy dog sidled in alongside the unsuspecting old lady. She wanted sausages and mince and goodness knows what else, so while the butcher was looking after her, the greedy dog pounced. He grabbed the steak and galloped out of the shop before anyone really had time to realise what was happening.

Then there was a great hue and cry. The butcher ran out of his shop with a bellow of rage, the little old lady fainted, and everyone in the street joined in the chase. But the greedy dog knew all the back streets, and he was soon far away and longing to eat his steak. He ran through the back streets until he came to the canal. He was just about to cross the bridge when he caught sight of another dog, right in front of him, and this dog also had a great juicy steak in his mouth! Well now, you and I know that what he was looking at was his own reflection, but the greedy dog did not know that. All he saw was a second steak that he might have so, with a great fierce bark, he leapt at the other dog.

But instead of gaining another meal, the greedy dog found himself very wet indeed, and he had lost his own steak! It would be good if I could tell you that from that day onwards the greedy dog was better behaved. But I am afraid his manners did not improve, and he is still looking for the other dog. . .

The Cat and the Mouse

a retelling from the original story by the Brothers Grimm

Now this is the tale of a wily cat and a foolish mouse. The mouse lived in a bare mouse hole under the pulpit in the church. The cat lived on an old cushion in the vestry. They had met on several occasions, the mouse usually whisking herself away very fast to the safety of her hole. She did not like the look of the cat's claws.

But one day, the cat called on the mouse at home.

"Miss mouse," a purry voice said, "why don't you and I set up home together? We could live in the bell tower and look after each other. We could share our food, too."

The mouse thought

about this carefully. She had never been fond of cats ever since her great grandfather had been supper for the farm tom cat one cold frosty night. But she could see that there would be benefits. The cat had a nice smile on his face. So she agreed.

They put their savings together and bought a pot full of fat for the winter. The cat said he would hide it away safely under the altar where no one ever went, and so it was done. They both promised not to touch it until the weather became really bad.

The mouse went about her business, quite happy in her new home, although she found the stairs a wearisome business. But the cat could not stop thinking about the pot of fat. So he thought up a plan.

"Miss mouse, my cousin has just had a kitten," he said looking at the mouse with his green eyes. "And she would like me to be godcat. I should like to go to the christening, would you mind?"

"Not at all, Mister cat," said the mouse. "I have plenty to do today."

But the wicked Cat went straight to the pot of fat and ate the top off. Then he went to sleep for the rest of the day. When it was evening, he stretched and strolled back up to the bell tower.

"Did you have a nice time?" asked the mouse

"Oh yes, very nice," said the not very nice cat.

"And what is the kitten called?"

"Topoff," replied the cat.

"Topoff?" asked the mouse. "That is a very strange name. Still I suppose cats have different family names," and she went on with her work.

All went quietly for a few days but then the cat had great longings for the pot of fat again so he went to the mouse.

"I find I have another new godkitten. Would you mind if I went to the christening?" said the cat, his green eyes half closed.

"Another godkitten?" said the mouse. "My, my you do have a big family."

And the beastly cat slunk off and ate up half the pot of fat. When he sauntered back up the stairs that night the mouse was waiting.

"Well, how did it all go?" she said. "What is this kitten to be called?"

"Halfempty," replied the cat.

"Halfempty?" said the mouse. "I have never heard such a thing before."

But the cat was asleep, a secret smile twitching his whiskers.

Well, as you can imagine, it was not long before that greedy cat wanted some fat again.

"Miss mouse, just imagine! I have yet another godkitten. I should really go to this christening too," said the cat.

Miss mouse thought it all very strange but she was a kindly creature so she waved the cat off to yet another christening. The cat, of course, just scuttled downstairs, slid under the altar and licked the pot of fat quite clean. He came back very late that night.

"Now what strange name did your family give this new kitten?" asked the mouse crossly. She had a headache from all the noise in the tower when the bells rang.

"Allgone," said the cat.

"Topoff, Halfempty and now Allgone!" the Mouse said

in disbelief. "Well, I am very glad I am not a member of your family. I couldn't be doing with such weird names," and she went to sleep with her paws over her ears.

There were no more christenings for a while. The weather became colder and colder, and the mouse began to think of the little pot of fat hidden under the altar.

"Mister cat," she said one frosty morning, "I think it is time we collected our pot of fat. I am looking forward to a lick."

We will see about that thought the cat, but he padded downstairs behind the mouse. She reached under the altar and brought out the pot, but of course when she looked in it was all empty.

"What a foolish mouse I have been!" she cried. "Now I see what a wicked cat you have been. Topoff, Halfempty and Allgone indeed!"

"Such is the way of cats," said the greedy cat, and he put out a paw to grab mouse. But she was too quick for him, and dived back into her dear little mouse hole under the pulpit.

Never again did she trust cats, ever, ever.

The Moon and Stars and Rainbows

The Star Maiden and the Flax Flowers

an Austrian fairytale

Peter the goatherd lived high up a mountainside with his mother in a little wooden house. A fast flowing river dashed down the valley, lush green meadows on either side. These meadows were full of flowers, bluebells, daisies and buttercups. In the summer, Peter took the goats even higher up into the mountains to the small patches of green grass that grew among the rocks. The goats wore bells round their necks, and all day long these bells would jingle as the goats leapt from rock to rock. In the evening, Peter would play his pipes and the goats would all gather round him for the journey back to the house and the barn where Peter's mother would milk them.

One evening as they all trotted back down into the

barn, Peter's mother called out to him.

"Where is the white nanny goat and her two kids?"

Peter looked round. They were not there.

"I saw them as we came down the valley, I will go and look for them," he said as he turned and blew his pipes again, calling over the meadow. But they did not appear. Peter set off up the mountain track again. He knew he had to find the goats before it grew too dark: climbing over the rocks would be a dangerous task with only the stars to guide his steps. He did not dare leave looking until the morning as he was afraid a wolf might snatch them away.

He climbed higher and higher, playing his pipes all the while, but he could not find a trace of the nanny goat and her kids. All night he searched without any luck. But in the summer the nights are not long, and just as he thought he could go no further, the rising sun tipped the mountain tops with pink. He sat down exhausted and closed his eyes for a moment. He heard the first calls of the birds as the light gradually crept over the grey rocks. And as he listened, he heard a soft voice calling his name.

"Peter, Peter," and with the

voice he heard a gentle bleating. He leapt to his feet and looked all round. He could see no sign of the goats. The voice came again.

"Peter, Peter," and as he looked up at the rocks above him, he saw a beautiful girl, dressed in a long blue cloak. Her eyes were blue too, as blue as the morning sky. She stood in front of a cave Peter could not remember seeing before. From underneath her cloak peeped the white nanny goat and her two kids.

"Call them, Peter," she said and he put the pipe to his lips and blew a joyous tune. The nanny goat and her two kids bounded down to stand by his side. Peter stroked their rough heads and looked up to the girl. She was so beautiful, he felt quite tongue-tied. She smiled at him and laughed gently.

"You are a good goatherd, Peter. I have watched over you and your herd for many a long day. When I found your nanny and her two kids last evening I brought them up here to keep them safe from the wild beasts through the night."

Peter was still silent. He was so overcome he couldn't even find the words to say thank you to the beautiful girl with the blue eyes. She beckoned him towards the cave.

"I should like to give you a gift to remember me by, Peter. Would you like to choose, look inside the cave," she said as she stood aside. Peter gasped. Inside the cave there were great mounds of precious stones, diamonds, rubies and emeralds. Peter finally found his tongue.

"Who are you?" he whispered.

"I am Hertha, the Star Maiden," the girl replied. "I look

after all the little ones, the kids, the lambs, the little rabbits and the birds in the air, the new leaves and flowers, even the babies in the cradles. Now Peter, all these precious stones come from deep inside the earth, so what will you have?"

"My mother and I have all we need. We have food and clothes and our little wooden house. We have our goats and their kids. We have no need of precious stones," Peter said proudly.

The girl seemed very pleased with this reply.

"Good, Peter! I am pleased to see you are content but I would still like to give you something."

Peter smiled shyly at her.

"I should like some of those beautiful blue flowers growing by the entrance to the cave."

Peter had never seen the flowers before, they had slender stems and sky blue flowers, just the colour of the girl's eyes. She clapped her hands in delight.

"That is my very own flower, Peter. It is called flax. I shall give you some seeds to sow as well and my flowers will bring much good to you and your people." And she gave Peter a handful of tiny golden seeds. As he looked at them lying in his hand, the girl's cloak billowed around her and she was gone. So was the cave with all the precious stones, but there at his feet was a bunch of the pale blue flowers. Peter and the goats went happily downhill back to the little wooden house where his mother was waiting anxiously for him.

Peter planted the golden seeds, and the next year the flax bloomed like a blue cloud in the valley. Then early one mid-summer morning, Hertha suddenly appeared and showed them how to dry and then comb the flax to make it into linen. And so the little blue flowers were indeed a gift that brought much good to everyone.

How Jumbo went to the Moon

an English tale first told by Joyce M Westrup 1936

Jumbo was a dog, a small woolly dog with a great plume of a tail. He belonged to two brothers who had decided after travelling the world that they wanted to settle down. So they looked for a place to build a house. They searched and searched and searched, and eventually they found just the right spot. They had discovered a little clearing in a great green forest, with a stream running by.

"This is the spot!" said the brothers to Jumbo and they all began work straight away on their new house. Jumbo didn't do very much other than run around barking, but he thought he was helping. The brothers cleared a big square in the grass, and then the eldest brother took his great axe and began chopping down a tall tree for the roof.

A huge great voice said, "Who said you could chop

down my trees?" and a big ugly face looked down at the brothers and Jumbo from above the tree. It was a giant, and he looked very cross.

"We wanted to build our new house here," said the younger brother bravely.

"Well, you can't!" said the giant and he stumped off back into the forest.

Now the brothers were very fed up at this turn of events. They had spent such a long time looking for a good place for their new house. They sat and thought what to do for ages. Jumbo helped them think by going to sleep. Then the elder brother said, "I have a splendid idea. Let's dig a very deep, deep pit and then cover it with branches so that when the giant comes along again he will fall into the pit and then we can build our house on top of him!"

So they set to, and Jumbo helped with the digging because he was good at that. Soon their giant trap was ready, and the elder brother took up his great axe again. He had only chopped his third chop when the giant came stomping down the path shouting at the top of his huge voice, "I thought I told you not to… HELP!" he yelled as he fell down the deep, deep pit. Well, it was a very deep, deep pit and the giant just could not get out. The two brothers cut down lots more trees and soon they had built a very nice house indeed, right over the deep, deep pit. They made a trap door in the kitchen floor so they could send down meals to the giant. The brothers were quite kind-hearted in this way, and it was the giant's forest after all.

Now the giant was quite well brought up, but the one thing he was very bad about was eating his crusts. He just dropped these onto the floor of the pit, and before long he was knee deep in crusts. Then he had a splendid idea.

He piled all the crusts up into one great heap, and when he climbed up this heap he found he could reach the trap door. He pushed the trap door open very carefully and scrambled out.

He found it was night-time and everybody, including Jumbo, was fast asleep. The giant bent down and scooped up the entire house in his great arms and he hurled it up, high, high into the sky. The two brothers landed on a star each, but Jumbo fell on the moon. They are all quite happy up there, and if you look very carefully sometimes you can see Jumbo, waving his great plume of a tail. I don't know what happened to the giant but I am sure it was a long time before anyone dared try to build a house in his forest again!

The Lad who went to the North Wind

a retelling from Popular Tales from the Norse by George Webbe Dasent

There was once a lad called Snorri who lived with his mother in the far north. They were very poor, and there was never very much food on the table. One day Snorri decided to visit the North Wind to see if he could do some work for him. But he was no good at huffing and puffing, and he couldn't blow big waves at sea, so the North Wind gave him a magic tablecloth.

"All you have to do is lay the cloth on the table and say, 'Cloth serve me, please!' and you will have food enough," said the North Wind.

Snorri thanked him very much and set off home. But it was soon dark so he stopped at an inn for the night. He spread the cloth out on a table and said, "Cloth serve me, please!" and there in a trice was enough food to feed everyone at the inn. All the other travellers were very grateful to Snorri, but the landlord saw a chance to make life easy for himself. When the lad was asleep, he stole the cloth and put an ordinary one in its place. Of course Snorri knew nothing of all this until he arrived home and tried to show his mother the North Wind's gift. Snorri decided to go back to the North Wind.

"That cloth you gave me didn't last very long," Snorri complained. "One meal and that was that."

Now the North Wind guessed what had happened so he gave Snorri another gift. This was a goose that would lay golden coins.

"All you have to say is, 'Goose fill my money bag, please!' and you will have plenty," said the North Wind.

Snorri thanked the North Wind and once again set off home, stopping at the same inn as before. He went into the stables to talk to the goose, but the landlord followed him and saw all that happened. Late at night, the landlord's wife put an ordinary goose in the place of the magic one. Of course Snorri knew nothing of all this until he arrived home. Snorri decided once again to go back to the North Wind.

"That goose you gave me didn't last very long," Snorri complained to the North Wind. "One bag of money and that was that."

The North Wind guessed what had happened so he gave Snorri a final gift. This was a stick that would beat whoever it was told to.

"All you have to say is, 'Beat, stick, beat, please!' and it will go on until you tell it to stop," said the North Wind.

So Snorri thanked the North Wind and set off home, visiting the same inn again. Snorri was not a foolish lad and he too had guessed that the landlord was the thief. So when he arrived at the inn, he made a great show of the stick and then lay down, pretending to sleep. The landlord found another stick and was just about

to change it for the North Wind's gift when Snorri sat up and shouted at the top of his voice, "Beat, stick, beat, please!" and the stick began to beat the landlord. Well, didn't he shout and didn't he roar! He ran round and round the room.

"Stop! Stop!" the landlord cried, but Snorri only laughed.

"Where is my tablecloth and my goose?" he shouted above the landlord's roars of pain. "If you give me my property back I will see if I can persuade the stick to stop."

"Please get your stick to stop beating my husband," the landlord's wife cried. "Here is your tablecloth and your goose," and she thrust them into Snorri's hands.

Only then did Snorri say, "Stop, stick, stop, please!"

The landlord disappeared very quickly, and so Snorri took up the stick and the tablecloth and he tucked the goose under his arm. He lived with his mother very comfortably ever after.

Kaatje's Treasure

a myth from Holland

Hans was a cheesemaker and he lived with his wife Kaatje. They had a small farm near the crossroads by the Old Inn outside the Dutch town of Haarlem. Every week Hans would go to market in Amsterdam with his great big round cheeses, and he would come back with some coins jingling in his pocket, and a few bulbs for his wife to plant in her little garden. Kaatje was a dreamer but Hans loved her very much.

One day as Hans was pressing the cheeses in the dairy, he noticed Kaatje was not singing as usual.

"What is wrong, my dear?" he asked. "You are not as happy as usual."

"Oh, husband, I have had a very strange dream three nights running now. It was so real!" she whispered.

"You and your dreams," laughed Hans. "Tell me what happened then."

So Kaatje told him that she had dreamt she must go to Amsterdam and then walk round the Corn Exchange three times. From then on she would be rich beyond her wildest dreams. Hans thought it was another of her daft wishes, but she was very serious so eventually he agreed to walk round the Corn Exchange three times when he next went to market with his cheeses. And so Kaatje would have to wait until market day. She simply couldn't wait that long so she crept out of the house very early the next morning while Hans was still asleep, and set off on the road to Amsterdam.

She walked and walked, and then some more and eventually she arrived in Amsterdam. She was very excited as she set off round the Corn Exchange. Once. Twice. And a final third time. Absolutely nothing happened. Kaatje sat down with a thump. Her feet were very sore. Her head ached. And she felt very silly. Whatever would Hans say when he heard where she had been. Her eyes filled with tears.

"Can I help you?" a kindly voice said. "You seem to be lost, I have watched you walk three times round the Corn Exchange."

Kaatje looked up and there was a man,

a farmer by the look of him, and he had such a kindly face that before too long Kaatje was telling him her silly dream. Well, he just laughed and laughed.

"I had a dream like that once, but I knew it was only a dream," the farmer said. "I dreamt I had to go to the dairy of a small farm near the crossroads by the Old Inn outside the Dutch town of Haarlem, and under the flagstones I would find a great chest of gold. Quite ridiculous! I think you should go home to your good husband and forget your dreams," and he walked away down the street.

Kaatje could not really believe what she had heard but tired as she was, she went home again as fast as ever she could.

Hans was cross with her at first for going on such a fool's errand, but when she demanded he dig up the dairy floor he just laughed at her. So she picked up the spade and began digging by herself.

The pile of earth grew higher and higher, and Hans despaired for his clean dairy. But then the spade struck something metal. Hans and Kaatje peered down into the hole.

An old rusting chest lay on its side, and spilling out was a great pile of coins! Well, then they both dug away with both hands and soon there was a great pile of gold coins on the dairy floor, enough to keep them in great comfort for the rest of their days. They were content with their way of life so they stayed at the farm near the crossroads by the Old Inn outside the Dutch town of Haarlem, and Hans went every week to market with his cheeses. But Kaatje never remembered a single one of her dreams ever again.

Snow-Daughter and Fire-Son

a German legend

There was once a husband and wife who had longed for many years to have a child. But as no child arrived they grew sad. One winter day they were outside clearing the snow away from their path. It had been bitterly cold, and there were huge icicles hanging off the roof. They sparkled in the sunlight. The wife turned to her husband and murmured,

"I wish I had as many children as there are icicles hanging from the roof."

When they turned to go back inside, the wife looked up again at the roof and sighed. As she did so, a tiny icicle fell from the roof and straight into her mouth.

"Ah, husband!" she laughed, "Perhaps now I will have a snow child!" and they thought no more of it.

But in the spring the following year, the wife did have a baby. It was a tiny girl whose skin was white as snow, and her eyes were like blue chips of ice. As the little girl grew, it was clear she never felt the cold. She would always run around with bare feet, and in the winter she would laugh and roll in the snow as soon as it fell. She hated the warmth, and would hide from the sun in the summer. Indoors, she would sit as far away from the fire as possible. Her mother and father called her Snow-daughter.

One winter's night when a blizzard was blowing, the man and his wife huddled by the fire.

"Ah, husband," said the wife, "perhaps it would have been better if I had produced a fire child," and as she spoke a spark flew from the fire into her lap.

The man laughed.

"You should not say things like that, wife. You never know what might happen."

In the spring the following year the wife produced a fine son with rosy cheeks and flashing black eyes. As the

little boy grew, he was always
complaining of the cold.

In the summer he would
dance in the heat of the sun,
and would stay outside
until the last rays had
dipped over the horizon.
His mother and father called
him Fire-son.

Now, of course, Fire-son and
Snow-daughter could not bear to be close to each other.
Fire-son would complain that Snow-daughter made him
shiver, and Snow-daughter would complain that Fire-son
made her skin burn.

Time passed. Fire-son grew into a fine, darkly
handsome young man, and Snow-daughter grew into a
beautiful shining fair young woman. Their mother and
father died, and Fire-son and Snow-daughter longed to
leave the little cottage and seek their fortunes. But they had
no one other than each other in the whole wide world and
they wished to travel together.

"I just know we should keep together if we are to be
lucky," said Snow-daughter.

"But how can we arrange it?" asked Fire-son. "If I stay
close to you my heart freezes, and if you come close to me
you burn from my heat."

Snow-daughter produced two huge fur cloaks. "If we

wear these we can walk side by side. I shall not feel your heat, and you will not feel my cold."

And so they set off. They travelled for many days, wandering far and wide, and saw many strange lands before they grew weary and decided to stop a while. Fire-son built himself a snug wooden hut where he always had a great fire burning, and Snow-daughter lived outside in the open air. When they met for supper, they would always put on the fur coats and sit outside.

One day they were sitting outside the hut together in their coats when the king and all his courtiers came by. He was captivated by Snow-daughter's beauty, and bade her tell him who she was and who the fiercely handsome young man in the fur coat was. And so they told the king the whole story. He wasted no time in asking Snow-daughter to marry him.

The king built a huge ice house underground for Snow-daughter, and he built a house inside a great oven for Fire-son. So they all lived happily ever after and, thankfully, when Snow-daughter gave birth to twins they seemed quite able both to sit by the fire and to dance in the snow!

The Moon Caught in the Marsh

a folk tale from East Anglia

The Moon looked down on the marsh. It was oozy and murky, and people were afraid to cross the marsh at night unless the Moon was shining. It was said that on dark nights the marsh goblins would lead travellers astray and drag them down into the clinging black mud.

Now the Moon did not believe these tales but she decided to see for herself. She wrapped herself in a great dark cloak and slipped down to the marsh. All you could see was her tiny silver feet below the cloak.

But the goblins could see in the dark. As soon as they saw the Moon's silver feet they all crept up close to her and tried to pull at the great cloak with their horrid cold hands. The Moon realised exactly what the travellers had to put up with. And then she heard a cry coming from quite close by. It was a poor man who had come to fetch the doctor for his wife who was going to have a baby. In the deep dark he had tripped over a tree root and hurt his foot.

The beastly goblins ran away from the Moon the moment they heard the man cry out and they began pushing and pulling him here, there and everywhere. The man yelled out in fear, and the Moon was so upset that she flung aside her cloak and shone out in all her bright glory. The goblins scattered, their eyes hurting from the brilliance of the Moon.

The man escaped from the marsh and ran all the way to the doctor, in the clear moonlight. And later that night, his wife safely produced a beautiful little girl with shining white hair. Everyone always said she looked like a moonbeam.

But the Moon was still in the marsh, and she found her tiny silver feet were stuck in the mud. She turned this way and that, but she could not get out. And then she stumbled and fell with a splash into the dark black mud. Instantly her glorious light went out. With wicked cries of delight the goblins all came running back, and rolled a great flat stone over the spot where the Moon lay trapped. Not a single beam of her light was to be seen.

Days went by, and then weeks. The villagers waited anxiously for the new Moon but there was no sign of it. When a month had gone by, several of the villagers gathered together to decide what to do. The man who had been rescued the night his daughter was born suggested that perhaps the Moon might be found near where he had been caught by the goblins. They set off towards the spot, bravely determined to find out what had happened to the Moon. They all carried flaring torches and sang bold songs to cheer themselves.

When they reached the spot the first thing they saw was the great flat stone. The next thing they saw was hundreds and hundreds of nasty spiteful goblins. The goblins tried to blow out the torches, but the men re-lit them as fast as ever possible. The men waded out into the marsh and with a huge effort lifted the side of the great stone. Out shone a blinding ray of moonlight. The goblins all disappeared, shrieking in dismay. Slowly, slowly the men lifted the stone and the grateful Moon sailed high into the sky once more. She shone down on the men as they walked home, and she shone the next night, and the next. Best of all, from that day forth there was never a goblin to be seen or heard in that part of the country.

The North Wind and the Sun

a retelling from Aesop's fables

The North Wind and the Sun once had a quarrel about who was the stronger. "I am stronger than you," said the North Wind. "I can blow down trees, and whip up great waves on the sea."

"I am stronger than you," said the Sun. "I can make flowers open, and turn fields of wheat from green to gold."

And so they argued back and forth, day after day. The East Wind and the Moon became very cross with them both and suggested that they have a competition to decide once and for all who was the strongest. A man was walking down the path, and he was wearing a big overcoat.

"Whichever one of you can first get that man to take off his coat is the strongest," said the Moon. And the East Wind said, "And then we will have no more quarrels!"

So the North Wind and the Sun agreed to the competition. The North Wind began. He blew and blew, the

coldest bitter wind he could manage. The great overcoat flapped round the man's legs as he struggled against the wind, but he only pulled the coat closer round his neck to keep out the bitter cold. Then it was the Sun's turn. She rose high in the sky and shone down on the man in the great overcoat. Warmer and warmer she shone, until the man unbuttoned the coat. Still the Sun beamed down, and finally the man flung off the coat, sweat pouring down his face. The Sun had won!

The North Wind blew off in a great huff, but he did not dare continue his quarrel with the Sun. So today when the fierce North Wind blows you have to remember that he is still very cross!

East of the Sun and West of the Moon

a retelling from Popular Tales from the Norse by George Webbe Dasent

Once there was a poor herdsman and his wife who lived in a tumbledown cottage in the north of the country with their family. There were seven sons and six daughters and the youngest daughter was the best of the lot.

One cold winter's night there came a gentle knock at the door. When the herdsman opened it, to his surprise there was a Great Brown Bear outside.

"Herdsman, I would be grateful if you would give me your youngest daughter," said the Brown Bear very politely. "If you do, I shall make you rich beyond belief."

This was a tempting offer, but the herdsman thought he should ask his daughter first. She said, "NO!" very loudly.

But the rest of the family persuaded her that the Brown Bear looked kind enough, and they really could do with the money. So she brushed her hair and put on her cloak, and

off she went with the Brown
Bear.

"Get on my back, and
hold onto my fur tightly," said
the Brown Bear, and she did.
They rode a long way to a
great castle. The Brown Bear
galloped in through the front
door, and there was a table laid
with a delicious-looking meal.
The Brown Bear gave the
daughter a silver bell saying,

"Whatever you want, just ring the bell and it shall be
yours," and he padded away silently.

Well, the youngest daughter ate till she was full and
then all she could wish for was a good sleep. So she rang
the silver bell, and she found herself in a warm room with a
great four poster bed. No sooner had she snuggled down in
the warm soft blankets and blown out the candle than she
felt something lie across her feet. It was the Brown Bear. But
when she woke in the morning he had gone. She rang her
bell for breakfast and then spent a very happy day
wandering round the castle.

And so she settled down to life in the Brown Bear's
castle. But after a while she grew sad. She missed her family.
So the Brown Bear offered to take her home for a visit. But
he warned her, "Whatever you do, you must not spend time
alone with your mother. If you do, there is no telling what

bad luck will follow."

She promised and they both set off. The Brown Bear bounded over the snow, and it seemed no time before she was once again with her family. They now lived in a grand house with many rooms and a servant for everyone. They all thanked her for making their lives so much happier.

Her mother said, "Now, my daughter, you must tell me all about your new life!" and she led her away from the rest of the family. The youngest daughter quite forgot her promise to the Brown Bear and she was soon telling her mother everything. When she came to the bit about the Brown Bear sleeping across her feet every night, her mother let out a great shriek.

"Foolish child! This bear must be a troll in disguise! You must wait until he is asleep, and then take a good look at him. Then you will see what he really is."

So when the Brown Bear had taken her home again, the youngest daughter did as her mother suggested. As she held the candle high above the bed she saw not a sleeping bear, not even a troll, but the most handsome prince ever. But, as she bent closer, some wax fell from the candle onto his shirt and he awoke with a start.

"Alas!" he cried. "What have you done? Had you only

waited, you might have released me from the wicked witch whose spell has turned me into a bear by day. Now I must return to her castle which is East O' the Sun and West O' the Moon, and marry the princess with the three-foot nose."

The prince looked at her once more, his eyes full of tears, and with a rumble of thunder he disappeared. As did the castle and the gardens. The youngest daughter found herself alone in the middle of a forest.

"Well, it is my fault that I have lost the prince so I will just have to try to find him again and rescue him," she said to herself, and she set off to find the castle East O' the Sun and West O' the Moon.

She had walked for seven days and seven nights when she met an old woman sitting by the roadside. The old woman had a golden apple in her lap.

"Do you know where I might find the castle East O' the Sun and West O' the Moon?" the girl asked.

The old woman replied, "No, but my sister might. You can borrow my horse, he will lead you to her. You better take this apple with you, too."

The horse galloped through the night for seven days until they saw an old, old woman sitting by the roadside. The old, old woman had a golden comb.

"Do you know where I might find the castle East O' the Sun and West O' the Moon?" the girl asked.

The old, old woman replied, "No, but my sister might. You can borrow my horse, he will lead you to her. You better take this comb with you, too."

The horse galloped through the night for seven days until they saw an old, old, old woman by the roadside. The old, old, old woman had a golden spinning wheel.

"Do you know where I might find the castle East O' the Sun and West O' the Moon?" the girl asked.

The old, old, old woman replied, "No, but the East Wind will. You can borrow my horse, he will lead you to him. You better take this spinning wheel with you, too."

The horse galloped through the night for seven days until they found the East Wind. He didn't know where the castle was. He suggested the girl try his brother the West Wind and he blew her all the way to the West Wind's house. But he didn't know where the castle was either. So the West

Wind suggested she try his brother the South Wind, but when they reached the South Wind's house he was fast asleep.

"I think you need to try my brother the North Wind, but he is very busy and very fierce," said the West Wind, and he blew her a long, long way to the top of a bleak mountain. There they met the North Wind.

"Do you know where I might find the castle East O' the Sun and West O' the Moon?" the girl asked.

"Indeed I do," howled the North Wind. "I will take you there," and with a mighty gust he blew the girl and the golden apple and the golden comb and the golden spinning wheel until they reached the castle East O' the Sun and West O' the Moon.

The girl sat down outside the castle and began to throw the golden apple high up into the air. A window was flung open and there stood the princess, her three-foot nose resting on the window edge.

"What do you want for your golden apple?" she shrieked down and her voice was like a saw.

"To spend the evening with the prince," replied the girl.

Well, that was easily arranged, but when she went into his chamber, the youngest daughter found the prince fast asleep. The witch had given him a sleeping draught so the youngest daughter went sadly away.

The next morning the girl sat combing her hair with the golden comb, and it was the same story. The princess with the three-foot nose took the golden comb, but again the prince just slept and slept.

The third morning, the youngest daughter sat outside with the golden spinning wheel, and again the princess stuck her great nose out of the window. But this time, the prince's little page told the prince all about the girl who had tried to wake him the nights before, so when the witch brought him his cocoa he only pretended to drink it.

When the youngest daughter came in, he was awake and waiting for her. As soon as he saw her, the prince was overjoyed and kissed her. Straightaway, there was a terrible shriek from the tower at the top of the castle as the witch disappeared in a flash of green light. The princess found her nose was three-foot longer again, so she ran away to hide and was never seen again.

The prince married the youngest daughter the very next day, and the castle East O' the Sun and West O' the Moon became a happy place. Even the North Wind blew more gently round the battlements.

The Little Boy's Secret

by David L Harrison

One day a little boy left school early because he had a secret to tell his mother. He was in a hurry to get home, so he took a short cut through some woods where three terrible giants lived. He hadn't gone far before he met one of them standing in the path.

When the giant saw the little boy, he put his hands on his hips and roared, "What are you doing here, boy? Don't you know whose woods these are?"

"I'm on my way home," answered the little boy. "I have a secret to tell my mother."

That made the giant furious. "Secret?" he bellowed. "What secret?"

"I can't tell you," said the little boy, "or it wouldn't be a secret any more."

"Then I'm taking you to our castle!" said the giant. Stooping down, he picked up the little boy and popped him into his shirt pocket.

Before long the first giant met a second giant who was twice as big, three times as ugly, and four times as fierce. "What's that in your pocket?" he asked the first giant.

"A boy," he answered. "Says he has a secret that he won't tell us."

When the second giant heard that, he laughed a wicked laugh.

"Won't tell us, eh?" he chuckled. "Well, we'll just see about that! To the castle with him!"

The giants thumped on down the path. In a short time they came to a huge stone castle beside a muddy river.

At the door they met the third giant, who was five

times bigger, six times uglier, and seven times fiercer than the second giant.

"What's that in your pocket?" he asked the first giant.

"A boy," he answered.

"A boy!" chuckled the third giant. He brought his huge eye close to the pocket and peered in.

"Says he has a secret he won't tell us," said the first giant.

When the third giant heard that, he laughed a terrible laugh. "Won't tell us, eh?" he asked. "Well, we'll just see about that! On the table with him!"

The first giant took the little boy from his pocket and set him on the kitchen table. Then all three giants gathered round and peered down at him.

The little boy looked at the first giant. He looked at the second giant. He looked at the third giant.

They were truly enormous and dreadful to behold.

"Well?" said the first giant.

"We're waiting," said the second giant.

"I'll count to three," said the third giant. "One…two…"

The little boy sighed a big sigh. "Oh, all right," he said. "I suppose I can tell you. But if I do, you must promise to let me go."

"We promise," answered the giants. But they all winked sly winks at one another and crossed their fingers behind their backs because they didn't really mean to let him go at all.

The little boy turned to the first giant. "Bend down," he said. The giant leaned down and the little boy whispered into his ear.

When the giant heard the secret, he leaped up from the table. His knees shook. His tongue hung out. "Oh, no!" he shouted. "That's terrible!" And he dashed from the castle, ran deep into the woods and climbed to the top of a tall tree. He didn't come down for three days.

The second giant scowled at the little boy.

"What's wrong with him?" he asked.

"Never mind," said the little boy. "Just bend down."

The giant leaned down and the little boy stood on tiptoe and whispered into his ear.

When the giant heard the secret, he leaped up so fast that he knocked his chair over. His eyes rolled. His ears twitched. "Let me get away," he roared. And he raced from the castle, ran over the hills and crawled into the deepest, darkest cave he could find.

The third giant frowned down at the little boy.

"What's wrong with them?" he asked.

"Never mind," said the little boy. "Just bend down."

The giant leaned down and the little boy climbed onto a teacup and whispered into his ear.

When the giant heard the secret, he jumped up so fast that he ripped the seat of his trousers. His teeth chattered. His hair stood on end. "Help!" he cried. "Help!" And he dashed from the castle and dived head first into the muddy river.

The castle door had been left open, and since the giants had promised the little boy that he could go, he walked out and went home.

At last he was able to tell his mother his secret; but she didn't yell and run away. She just put him to bed and gave him some supper.

The next morning when the little boy woke up, he was covered from head to toe with bright red spots.

"Now I can tell everybody what my secret was," he said with a smile. "My secret was…I'M GETTING THE MEASLES!"

The Sorcerer's Apprentice

a German folk tale

The sorcerer lived in a dusty room at the top of a very tall gloomy tower. His table was covered with bottles and jars full of strange-coloured potions, and bubbling mixtures filled the air with horrible smells. The walls of the tower were lined with huge old books. These were the sorcerer's spell books and he would let no one else look inside them.

The sorcerer had a young apprentice called Harry. He was a good but lazy boy who longed only to be able to do magic himself. The sorcerer had promised to teach him all he knew, but only when he thought Harry was ready.

One day the sorcerer had to visit a friend who was a warlock. The sorcerer had never left Harry alone in the tower before and he did not entirely trust him. Looking very fierce, the sorcerer gave Harry his instructions.

"I have a very important spell to conjure up tonight when I return, so I need the cauldron full of water from the well," he said. "When you have filled the cauldron, you can sweep the floor and then you must light the fire."

Harry was not best pleased. It would take many, many trips to the well to fill the cauldron, and he would have all those steps to climb each time. Perhaps the sorcerer could read his mind, for the last thing he said as he climbed out of the window to fly away on his small green dragon was, "Touch nothing!" and off he flew in a cloud of smoke and flame from the dragon.

Harry watched until the sorcerer was safely far out of sight, and then did precisely what he had been told not to do. He took down one of the old dusty spell books. For a while all was quiet in the tower, and then Harry found what he was looking for. It was a spell to make a broomstick obey orders. Harry didn't hesitate. He forgot the sorcerer's instructions, he forgot that magic can be very dangerous. He took the broomstick in one hand and the spell book in the other, and read out the spell in a quavery voice for, truth to tell, he was very nervous. Nothing happened. Harry tried again, and this time his voice was stronger.

The broomstick quivered and then stood up. It grabbed a bucket and jumped off down the stairs. Soon it was back, the bucket brimful of water which it tipped into the cauldron. Harry was delighted and smiled as the broomstick set off down the stairs again. Up and down the broomstick went and soon the cauldron was full.

"Stop, stop!" shouted Harry, but the broomstick just carried on, and on. Soon the floor was awash and then the bottles and jars were floating around the room. Nothing Harry could say would stop the broomstick, and so in desperation, he grabbed the axe that lay by the fireside and chopped the broomstick into pieces. To his horror, all the pieces of wood turned into new broomsticks and they set off downstairs to the well, buckets appearing magically in their hands.

By now the water was nearly up to the ceiling. Wet spell books spun round and round the room, and Harry gave himself up for lost. Suddenly there was a great clatter of wings and a hiss of steam as the green dragon flew into the tower. The sorcerer was back! In a huge voice he commanded the broomsticks to stop. They did. Then he ordered the water back into the well. It all rushed back down the stairs. Then he ordered the dragon to dry everything with its hot breath. Then he turned to look at Harry. And, oh dear! Harry could see that the sorcerer was very, very angry indeed. The sorcerer looked as if he might turn Harry into something terrible, but then he sat down on a soggy cushion with a squelch.

"Right, I think it is time I taught you how to do magic PROPERLY!" And he did.

Goldilocks and the Three Bears

a retelling from the original tale by Andrew Lang

O nce upon a time there was a little girl called Goldilocks who lived in the middle of a great forest with her mother and her father. Now ever since she was tiny, her mother had told her she must never, ever wander off into the forest for it was full of wild creatures, especially bears. But as Goldilocks grew older she longed to explore the forest.

One washday, when her mother was busy in the kitchen, hidden in clouds of steam, Goldilocks sneaked off down the path that led deep into the forest.

At first she was happy, looking at the wild flowers and listening to the birds singing, but it did not take long for her to become hopelessly lost.

She wandered for hours and hours and, as it grew darker, she became frightened. She started to cry, but then she saw a light shining through the trees. She rushed forward, sure she had somehow found her way home, only to realise that it was not her own cottage that she was looking at. But she opened the door and looked inside.

On a scrubbed wooden table there were three bowls of steaming hot porridge; a big one, a middle-sized one and a little one. Goldilocks was so tired that she quite forgot all her manners and just sat down at the table. The big bowl was too tall for her to reach. The middle-sized bowl was too hot. But the little one was just right, so she ate all the porridge up.

By the warm fire there were three chairs: a big one, a middle-sized one and a little one. Goldilocks couldn't climb up into the big one. The middle-sized one was too hard. The

little was just the right size, but as soon as she sat down, it broke into pieces. Goldilocks scrambled to her feet and then noticed there were steps going upstairs, where she found three beds: a big one, a middle-sized one and a little one. The big bed was too hard. The middle-sized one was too soft. But the little one was just right and she was soon fast asleep.

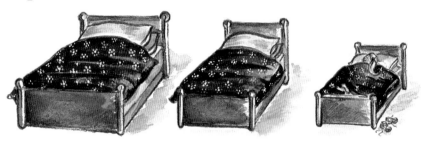

The cottage belonged to three bears, and it was not long before they came home. They knew at once that someone had been inside.

Father Bear growled,

"Who has been eating my porridge?"

Mother Bear grumbled,

"Who has been eating my porridge?"

And Baby Bear gasped,

"Who has been eating my porridge, AND has eaten it all up?"

The bears looked round the room. They looked at the chairs by the warm fire.

Father Bear growled,

"Who has been sitting in my chair?"

Mother Bear grumbled,

"Who has been sitting in my chair?"

And Baby Bear gasped,

"Who has been sitting in my chair, AND has broken it to bits?"

The bears all clumped upstairs. They looked at the three beds.

Father Bear growled,

"Who has been sleeping in my bed?"

Mother Bear grumbled,

"Who has been sleeping in my bed?"

And Baby Bear gasped,

"Who has been sleeping in my bed, AND is still there?"

Suddenly Goldilocks woke up. All she could see was three very cross-looking bears. She jumped off the bed, ran down the stairs, and out of the door. She ran and ran and ran, and by good fortune found herself outside her own cottage. Her mother and father scolded, but then gave her lots of hugs and kisses, and a big bowl of soup. Goldilocks had certainly learnt her lesson, and she never ever wandered off again.

Peter and the Wolf

original libretto by Sergey Prokofiev

Peter lived with his grandfather at the edge of the forest. Peter used to play with the wild birds and animals in the garden, but his grandfather always warned him not to go into the meadow in case the wolf crept out of the forest.

I am afraid Peter did not always do as he was told, so one day he slipped through the garden gate and into the meadow when he met a duck swimming in the middle of the pond.

"You must watch out for the wolf," said Peter to the duck but she was too busy enjoying herself to listen. Round and round the pond she swam. A little bird flew

down and the duck tried to persuade her to come into the pond as well. But as the little bird stood talking to the duck, Peter saw the cat sneak up behind her.

"Look out!" shouted Peter and the bird flew up to safety in the tree.

"Thank you, Peter," she said. The cat was not so pleased. Just then Peter's grandfather came out and saw the open garden gate.

"Peter! How many times do I have to tell you? Come back into the garden at once," he shouted and Peter walked slowly back in.

Meanwhile, at the far side of the meadow, nearest the forest, a grey shape slunk out from under the trees. It was the wolf!

The little bird flew up into the tree, and the cat joined her, although on a lower branch. But the duck was too busy swimming to see what was happening and in a flash the wolf grabbed her and swallowed her whole!

Peter saw it all from the garden.

"I am going to catch that old wolf," he said to himself.

He found a piece of rope and climbed up a tree whose branches overhung the meadow. He made a loop in the rope and hung it out of the tree. Then he called to the little bird, "Can you tempt the

wolf this way by flying round his head, please? I am going to catch him!"

The brave little bird darted down very close to the wolf's nose. The wolf snapped his fierce teeth, and only just missed the little bird. Closer and closer they came to the tree where Peter was hiding. The wolf was so busy trying to catch the bird that he did not see the rope. Peter looped it over the wolf's tail, and there he was, dangling from the branch of the tree!

Peter's grandfather came out and he was astonished to see the wolf. Just then some hunters came out of the forest.

"Well done," they cried, "you have caught the wolf. We have been after him for a long time."

And they all went off in a very joyful procession to the zoo. Peter led the wolf at the front, the little bird flew overhead, and the cat padded alongside, taking care not to get too close to the wolf. The hunters came up in the rear with Peter's grandfather. And from deep inside the wolf's tummy, the duck quacked loudly, just to remind everyone that she was there!

The Wiggly Tooth

by Dorothy Edwards

When I was a little girl, and my naughty little sister was a very little girl, we used to have an apple tree in our garden, and sometimes my naughty little sister used to pick the apples and eat them. It was a very easy thing to do because the branches were so low.

So, my mother told us we were not to pick the apples. My mother said, "It is naughty to pick the apples when they are growing upon the tree, because we want them to go on growing until they are ripe and rosy, and then we shall pick them and put them quite away for the winter-time."

"If you want an apple," my mother said, "you must pick up a windfall and bring it to me, and I will wash it for you."

As you know, 'windfalls' are apples that fall off the tree onto the grass, so one day, my little sister looked under the

tree and found a nice big windfall on the grass, and she took it in for my mother to wash.

When my mother had washed the apple, and cut out the specky bit where a little maggot had gone to live, my little sister sat down on the step to eat her big apple.

She opened her mouth very wide, because it was such a big apple, and she took a big bite. And what do you think happened? She felt a funny cracky sort of feeling in her mouth. My naughty little sister was so surprised that she nearly tumbled off the step when she felt the funny cracky feeling in her mouth, and she put in her finger to see what the crackiness was, and she found that one of her nice little teeth was loose.

So my naughty little sister ran indoors to my mother, and she said, "Oh, dear, my tooth has gone all loose and wiggly, what shall I do?" in a waily whiny voice because at first she didn't like it very much.

My mother said, "There's nothing to worry about. All your nice little baby-teeth will come out one by one to make room for your big grown-up teeth."

"Have a look, have a look," said my naughty little sister. So my mother had a look, and then she said, "It's just as I thought, there is a new little tooth peeping through already."

So after that my little sister had a loose tooth, and she used to wiggle it and wiggle it with her finger. She used to wiggle it so much that the tooth got looser and looser.

When the nice baker came, my naughty little sister showed him the tooth, and she showed the milkman and the window-cleaner man, and sometimes she used to climb up to the mirror and wiggle it hard, to show herself, because she thought that a loose tooth was a very special thing to have.

After a while, my mother said, "Your tooth is so very loose, you had better let me take it out for you."

But my naughty little sister didn't want to lose her lovely tooth, because she liked wiggling it so much, and she wouldn't let my mother take it out at all.

Then my mother said, "Well, pull it out yourself then," and my silly little sister said, "No, I like it like this."

The next time the window-cleaner man came, he said, "Isn't that toothy-peg out yet?"

And my naughty little sister said, "No. It's still here." And she opened her mouth very wide to show the window-cleaner man that it was still there.

The window-cleaner man said, "Why don't you pull it out? It's hanging on a threddle, it is indeed."

My naughty little sister told him that she liked to have it wiggle and to show people.

So the window-cleaner man said, "You'd better take it to show the dentist."

My naughty little sister said why should she take it to the dentist? Because she hadn't heard much about dentists, and the window-cleaner man who knew all about doctors and dentists and about how the sun moves and how pumpkins grow, told my naughty little sister all about dentists, how they looked after people's teeth for them, and made teeth for grown-up people who hadn't any of their own.

The window-cleaner man told my naughty little sister that his teeth were dentist-teeth and they were much prettier than his old ones, and my naughty little sister was very interested, and she said she would like the dentist to see her wiggly tooth.

So, the next time my mother said, "What about that tooth, now?" my naughty little sister said, "I want to go to the dentist."

My mother said, "Goodness me, surely it's loose enough for you to pull out yourself now?"

But my naughty little sister started to cry, "I want to go to the dentist. I want to go, I do," in a miserable voice like that.

So my mother said, "Very well then. I want the dentist to see your teeth anyway, so we shall go as soon as he can see you!"

Well now, the dentist was a very nice man; he said he thought he'd really better see my naughty little sister's tooth right away.

When my mother and my little sister arrived at the dentist's they had to wait in the waiting-room with a lot of other people. My naughty little sister told all these other people about her wiggly tooth, and she showed it to them, and they all said what a lucky child she was to have such a wiggly tooth.

When it was my naughty little sister's turn to see the dentist, she was very pleased. She sat on his big chair and let him have a good look.

The dentist said, "It's a very nice tooth, old lady. I'm sorry you don't want it taken out."

168

"I want it to wiggle with," said my silly little sister. Then my little sister asked all about making teeth and everything, and the dentist told her very nicely.

"It's a pity you don't want to part with that tooth though," he said, "because I should just like a tooth like that for my collection. I collect really nice teeth," the dentist said.

My naughty little sister thought and thought, and she couldn't help seeing how very nice it would be to have a tooth in a real collection, so, do you know what she did? She put her hand up to her mouth, as quick as quick, and then she said, "Here you are," and there, right in the middle of her hand was her little tooth. She'd pulled it out all her very self.

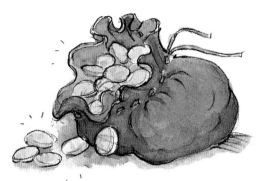

Dick Whittington and his Cat

an English myth

Hundreds of years ago there lived a poor orphan boy called Dick Whittington. His only possession was his cat, but everyone in his village looked after him, so he never wanted for a meal or clothes on his back. In return, he worked hard wherever he was needed. Now Dick's greatest dream was to visit the great city of London where, he had heard, the streets were paved with gold.

One day, a waggoner pulled into the village to give his two great shire horses a drink. Dick offered to rub the horses down, and before long he was telling the waggoner all about his dreams of visiting London town.

"Well, you must be in luck today," smiled the waggoner, "for that is where I am bound. Why don't you come with me and I will drop you off back here again when I return tomorrow?"

This was too good
an offer to refuse, so Dick
and his cat waved
goodbye to the villagers
and set off with the
waggoner for London.
When they arrived, Dick
looked round about in
astonishment. Never
before had he seen such
huge buildings, all
crowded so closely
together. And there were
so many people! Dick
set off to explore,
promising the waggoner
he would be back in the evening.

The pavements certainly did not appear to be made of
gold. But he kept on thinking he should just try round the
next corner, and then the next and, before long, Dick
realised that he was hopelessly lost. He stumbled into a
doorway, and worn out with hunger and worry at not
keeping his promise to help the waggoner, he fell fast asleep.

Now as luck would have it, Dick had chosen a very
good doorway to sleep in. The house belonged to a rich
merchant, Mr Fitzwarren, who was very kind and always
willing to help anyone in need. So when he came home

later that evening, Mr Fitzwarren took Dick and his cat indoors and told the cook to give him supper. The cook was very grumpy indeed at having to prepare a meal late at night for Dick who, she thought, looked like a ragamuffin.

The next morning, Dick told Mr Fitzwarren the whole story. Smiling, Mr Fitzwarren told Dick that, as he had found, the streets of London were not paved with gold, and indeed life there was very hard.

"But you look like a strong boy, would you like to work for me, Dick?" he asked. "You will have a roof over your head and a good dinner every day in return for helping in the kitchen and the stables."

Dick was delighted, and he soon settled into the household. He worked hard, and everyone liked him, except the cook. She gave him all the really horrible jobs in the kitchen and would never let him have a moment's rest. But she didn't dare defy her master and so Dick had his good dinner every day.

Now whenever one of Mr Fitzwarren's ships went to sea, it was his custom to ask everyone in the household to give something to the ship's cargo for luck. Poor Dick had only his cat and it was with a very heavy heart that he handed her over.

The ship was at sea for many, many months before they finally came to port in China. The captain and the crew went ashore to show the emperor the cargo they had brought all the way from London. The emperor had known

the captain for many years and they were old friends, so they sat down to a state banquet before discussing business. But to the emperor's great embarrassment, the entire meal was ruined by the rats that boldly ran everywhere, even over the plates they were eating off. The emperor explained that they had tried everything but nothing could rid the court of the plague of rats. The captain smiled.

"I think I have the answer," he said and he sent for Dick's cat. Within moments of her arrival, there were piles of dead rats at the emperor's feet. He was so impressed that he gave the captain a ship full of gold just for the cat.

Back in London, Dick's life was a misery. The cook was nastier than ever and he didn't even have his beloved cat for company, so one day he ran away, intending to walk home to his village. But he had not gone far before he heard the church bells ringing, and they seemed to say,

"Turn again Dick Wittington,
Thrice Lord Mayor of London."

Dick didn't know what the bells
meant, but he remembered how
kind Mr Fitzwarren had been, so
he turned round again and
went back before the cook
had even noticed that he
was missing. Of course
when the ships came home,
Mr Fitzwarren gave Dick his
fair share and more. This was the
start of Dick's prosperity, and he
even married Mr Fitzwarren's
daughter, Jane. He did become
Lord Mayor of London three
times, but he never forgot
his early days of
poverty and he founded
schools and hospitals for
the poor. He and
Jane had many
children, and
there were
always lots of
cats in their great
house as well!

The Precious Stove

an Austrian folk tale

Peter lived with his mother and father and his brothers and sisters in an old wooden cottage deep in the woods of Austria. They were very poor and the cottage had hardly any furniture, and they might have been very cold in winter were it not for their most treasured possession, a stove. This was no ordinary stove. It was made of white porcelain and it was so tall the gold crown at the top almost scraped the ceiling. Its feet were carved like lion's claws, the talons painted gold. The sides of the stove were painted with flowers and rare birds, in glowing colours, and the door was tiled in blue and gold. It looked very out of place in the poor wooden cottage for it had originally been made for a king's palace. Many years before, Peter's grandfather had rescued it, after a great war, from the ruins of the palace where he used to work. Peter used to draw copies of the flowers and birds on pieces of brown paper with a stub of old pencil.

One evening, as Peter and his sister Gilda lay curled up in the warmth at the foot of the stove, their father came in, shaking the snow from his boots. He looked tired and ill.

"My children, this is the last night you will be able to enjoy our beautiful stove," he said sadly. "Tomorrow it will be taken away as I have had to sell it. We have no money left, and we need food more than we need a grand stove."

The children were horrified, but their father would not change his mind. That night, instead of banking up the stove to keep it burning warmly through the night, he let the fire die down so it was quite cold in the morning. The traders arrived and loaded the stove onto a cart, and off it rumbled down the track towards the town. Peter's mother and father looked at the handful of gold coins the traders had given them and shook their heads. It seemed a poor bargain when all was said and done.

Peter and Gilda whispered together outside behind the wood pile.

"You have to follow the cart, Peter," said Gilda, "so you can see where our stove goes."

So Peter rushed off down the track after the cart, pausing only to stuff a couple of apples into his pocket. The journey into town was slow as the stove was heavy so the cart could not travel very fast, but by evening it had reached the station. Peter crept as close as he dared, and heard the traders arranging for the stove to go to Vienna by train the very next morning. He made up his mind very quickly. Once the traders had gone to an inn for the night, he clambered up and inside the stove. There was plenty of room inside for a small boy, and he knew that air would come in from the grill at the top under the golden crown. He soon fell fast asleep.

When he awoke, the train was moving fast. It sped through snowy forests and past the mighty Danube river. Peter munched his apples and wondered what his parents

would be thinking, and just where was he going to end up, and then what could he do, anyway, to keep the stove for his family.

Eventually the train came to a halt and with much banging and clattering all the boxes around the stove were unloaded onto the platform. Then Peter heard a gruff voice.

"Have a care there! That valuable stove is going to the palace, take care it isn't damaged in any way or it will be the worse for you!"

The palace! Peter's knees shook. The palace, why that was where the king lived. Peter sat as quiet as a mouse as he felt the stove lifted up off the train and onto another cart. It clattered through cobbled streets and over a wooden bridge, and then came to a halt. Many voices came through the grill as the stove was moved off the cart.

"My word, the king will be pleased! Look what a fine stove it is," said one voice.

"It must have come from a palace originally, look at the golden crown at the top," said another.

Then there was silence for a while. Peter strained his ears, and his knees shook a little more. Then he heard the swishing of long robes on a polished floor, and a murmur of voices. Then a deep hush.

"Truly, it is a very beautiful stove. I did not expect it to be so fine. Look at the quality of the painting round the sides," said a deep important voice. And then the handle of the door turned and light flooded into the stove. Peter tumbled out onto the floor as the same deep voice said, "Good gracious! What have we here, there is a child in the stove!"

Peter picked himself up and looked up into eyes that were full of laughter. They belonged to a man dressed in a bright red jacket with great gold tassels and gold buttons. Many glittering medals gleamed on his chest. A great silver sword hung by his side. It was the king!

Peter was absolutely terrified, but the king kept on smiling.

"Well, my boy, would you like to tell me how you come to be inside my new stove?"

A servant rushed forward and grabbed Peter by the arm, meaning to drag him away, but the king raised his hand and the man stepped back.

"Let the child speak," said the king.

Well, once Peter found his tongue, he could not stop. He told the king all about the stove. How it had stood in their poor cottage for as long as he could remember. How much the family welcomed its heat in the winter. And he told the

king that his father had been forced to sell the stove for a few gold pieces to buy food.

The king listened in silence while Peter told his story.

"Peter, I am not going to give you back your stove for it belongs here in the palace, but I will give your father several bags of gold, for it is a very valuable stove. And perhaps you would like to stay here and look after it for me?" he asked.

Peter was delighted. And he looked after the stove for the king from that day on. His family never wanted for food again, and every summer they would all come to stay at the palace to see Peter, and the stove of course. When the king discovered how good Peter was at drawing, he sent him to art school and he became a very fine artist. But when he was an old man, all his grandchildren wanted to hear was the story of how he came to Vienna inside a stove!

Little Red Riding Hood

a retelling from the original tale by Charles Perrault

There was once a little girl who lived in the middle of a deep dark forest with her mother and father, who was a woodcutter. The little girl always wore a red cloak with a warm hood and so she was called Little Red Riding Hood.

One day she decided to visit her granny who lived some way from the woodcutter's cottage. She took a basket with a cake her mother had baked and set off. Now the last thing her mother had said to Little Red Riding Hood was, "Don't leave the path, and don't talk to any strangers," but I am afraid Little Red Riding Hood was not really listening. So when

she saw some bluebells growing under a tree she left the path and began to pick a bunch for her granny. Slowly, slowly she wandered further away from the path, deeper into the trees. Suddenly, she was not alone. There in front of her stood a great big wolf. Now Little Red Riding Hood had not met a wolf before so she did not realise that wolves are not the kind of people it is wise to be too friendly with.

"Good day, little girl," said the wolf with a snarly sort of a smile. "What is your name and where are you going?"

"My name is Little Red Riding Hood. I am going to visit my granny, and I am taking her a cake to eat," replied Little Red Riding Hood.

The wolf was delighted. Not only a little girl to eat but a granny AND a cake as well!

"And where does your granny live, little girl?" asked the wolf, trying very hard to smile nicely despite all his fierce teeth.

Little Red Riding Hood told the wolf where her granny lived, and went on picking bluebells. The wolf slipped away through the trees and soon found the granny's cottage. He tapped on the door and said, in a disguised voice, "Hello, granny. It is Little Red Riding Hood. I have brought you a cake, will you let me in?"

As soon as the door was open, the wolf bounded in, and gobbled the granny all up! He put on her nightcap and shawl and climbed into her bed. Soon he heard Little Red Riding Hood coming and he tried his snarly smile again.

"Hello, granny," said Little Red Riding Hood. "I have brought you a cake and these bluebells," and she came up to the bedside.

"Goodness, granny! What great big eyes you have!" she said.

"All the better to see you with," growled the wolf. Little Red Riding Hood could not help noticing the wolf's teeth.

"Goodness, granny! What great big teeth you have!"

"All the better to eat you with!" snapped the wolf and gobbled Little Red Riding

Hood up. He gobbled up the cake in the basket as well and then, very full indeed, he fell fast asleep, snoring loudly.

Now by great good luck, Little Red Riding Hood's father was passing by the cottage, and when he heard the terrible snores he put his head round the door to see who was making such a noise. He was horrified to see the wolf so he took his axe and made a great slit down the wolf's tummy. Out jumped Little Red Riding Hood. Out staggered granny. She stitched up the wolf's tummy and told him to mind his manners in future. Then, as there was no cake left for tea, they all went back home, and Little Red Riding Hood's mother made pancakes. I am pleased to say Little Red Riding Hood had learnt her lesson, and she never spoke to wolves again.

The Gingerbread Boy

an English folk tale

One fine sunny day, an old woman was making some ginger biscuits. She had a little dough left over and so she made a gingerbread boy. She gave him two raisins for eyes and three cherries for buttons, and put a smile on his face with a piece of orange peel. And she popped him in the oven. But as she lifted the tray out of the oven when the biscuits were cooked, the gingerbread boy hopped off the tray and ran straight out of the door! The old woman ran after him, and her husband ran after her, but they couldn't catch the gingerbread boy. He called out, "Run, run, as fast as you can! You can't catch me, I'm the gingerbread man!"

The old dog in his kennel ran after the old man and the old woman, but he couldn't catch the

gingerbread boy. The ginger cat, who had been asleep in the sun, ran after the dog, but she couldn't catch the gingerbread boy. He called out,

"Run, run, as fast as you can! You can't catch me, I'm the gingerbread man!"

The brown cow in the meadow lumbered after the cat, but she couldn't catch the gingerbread boy. The black horse in the stable galloped after the cow but he couldn't catch the gingerbread boy. He called out,

"Run, run, as fast as you can! You can't catch me, I'm the gingerbread man!"

The fat pink pig in the sty trotted after the horse, but she couldn't catch the gingerbread boy. The rooster flapped and squawked after the pig but he couldn't catch the gingerbread boy. He called out,

"Run, run, as fast as you can! You can't catch me, I'm the gingerbread man!"

He ran and ran, and the old woman and the old man, the dog and the cat, the cow and the horse, the pig and the rooster all ran after him. He kept on running until he came to the river. For the first time since he had hopped out of the oven, the gingerbread boy had to stop running.

"Help, help! How can I cross the river?" he cried.

A sly fox suddenly appeared by his side.

"I could carry you across," said the sly fox.

The gingerbread boy jumped onto the fox's back, and the fox slid into the water.

"My feet are getting wet," complained the gingerbread boy.

"Well, jump onto my head," smiled the fox, showing a lot of very sharp teeth. And he kept on swimming.

"My feet are still getting wet," complained the gingerbread boy again after a while. "Well, jump onto my nose," smiled the fox, showing even more very sharp teeth.

The gingerbread boy jumped onto the fox's nose, and SNAP! the fox gobbled him all up. When the fox climbed out of the river on the other side, all that was left of the naughty gingerbread boy was a few crumbs. So the old woman and the old man, the dog and the cat, the cow and the horse, the pig and the rooster all went home and shared the ginger biscuits. They were delicious.

Jack and the Beanstalk

a retelling from the original tale by Joseph Jacobs

This is the story of how Jack did a silly thing, but all was well in the end.

Jack and his mother were very poor and there came a sad day when there was just no more money left, so Jack's mother told him to take the cow to market and sell her.

As Jack led the cow to market, he met a funny little man with a tall feather in his hat.

"And where might you be going with that fine-looking cow?" the funny little man asked.

Jack explained and the funny little man swept off his hat with the tall feather, and shook out five coloured beans.

"Well, young Jack, I can save you a journey. I will give

you these five magic beans in exchange for your cow."

Now Jack should have realised that this was all rather odd, for how did the funny little man know his name? But once he heard the word "magic" he didn't stop to think. He took the beans at once, gave the funny little man the cow and ran off home to his mother.

"Jack, you are a complete fool! You have exchanged our fine cow for five worthless beans!" She flung the beans out of the window, and sent Jack to bed without any supper.

When he woke in the morning, Jack couldn't understand why it was so dark in the cottage. He rushed outside to find his mother staring in amazement at the most enormous beanstalk that reached right up into the clouds.

"I told you they were magic beans," smiled Jack, and without any hesitation he began to climb the beanstalk. He climbed and climbed until he could no longer see the ground below. When he reached the top there stood a vast castle. Jack knocked at the door, and it was opened by a HUGE woman!

Boys and Girls

"My husband eats little boys for breakfast so you better run away quickly," she said to Jack. But before Jack could reply, the ground started to shake and tremble.

"Too late!" said the giant's wife. "You must hide," and she bundled Jack into a cupboard. Jack peeped through the keyhole, and saw the most colossal man stump into the kitchen.

"Fee fi fo fum! I smell the blood of an Englishman!" he roared.

"Don't be silly, dear. You can smell the sausages I have just cooked for your breakfast," said the giant's wife, placing a plate piled high with one hundred and sixty-three sausages in front of him. The giant did not seem to have very good table manners, and had soon gobbled the lot. Then he poured a great bag of gold onto the table, and counted all the coins.

190

With a smile on his big face, he soon fell asleep.

Jack darted out of the cupboard, grabbed the bag of money and hared out of the kitchen. He slithered down the beanstalk as fast as ever he could and there, still standing at the bottom, was his mother. She was astonished when she saw the gold.

Jack's mother bought two new cows and she and Jack were very content now they had plenty to eat every day. But after a while Jack decided he would like to climb the beanstalk again. The giant's wife was not very pleased to see him.

"My husband lost a bag of gold the last time you were here," she muttered looking closely at Jack, but then the ground began to shake and tremble. Jack hid in the cupboard again.

The giant stumped into the kitchen.

"Fee fi fo fum! I smell the blood of an Englishman!" he roared.

"Don't be silly, dear. You can smell

the chickens I have just cooked for your breakfast," said the giant's wife, placing a plate piled high with thirty-eight chickens in front of him. The giant had soon gobbled the lot. Then he lifted a golden hen onto the table, and said, "Lay!" and the hen laid a golden egg. With a smile on his big face he fell asleep, snoring loudly.

Jack darted out of the cupboard, grabbed the golden hen and hared out of the kitchen. He slithered down the beanstalk as fast as ever he could and there, still standing at the bottom, was his mother. She was astonished when she saw the hen.

Jack's mother bought a whole herd of cows and found a farmer to look after them. She bought lots of new clothes for herself and Jack, and they were very content. But after a while Jack decided he would like to climb the beanstalk one last time. The giant's wife was not at all pleased to see him.

"My husband lost a golden hen the last time you were here," and she peered closely at Jack, but then the ground began to shake and tremble. This time Jack hid under the table.

The giant stumped into the kitchen.

"Fee fi fo fum! I smell the blood of an Englishman!" he roared.

"I would look in the cupboard if I were you," said the giant's wife, but of course the cupboard was empty. They were both puzzled. The giant trusted his nose, and his wife didn't know where Jack had gone.

"Eat your breakfast, dear. I have just cooked you ninety-two fried eggs," said the giant's wife, placing a plate in front of him. The giant had soon gobbled the lot. Then he lifted a golden harp onto the table, and said, "Play!" and the harp played so sweetly that the giant was soon fast asleep, snoring loudly.

Jack crept out from under the table and grabbed the golden harp, but as soon as he touched it the harp called out, "Master, master!" and the giant awoke with a great start. He chased after Jack who scrambled down the beanstalk as fast as ever he could with the harp in his arms. As soon as Jack reached the ground he raced to get a big axe and chopped through the beanstalk. Down tumbled the great beanstalk, down tumbled the giant and that was the end of them both!

Jack and his mother lived very happily for the rest of their days. The bag of gold never ran out, the hen laid a golden egg every day, and the harp soon forgot about the giant and played sweetly for Jack and his mother.

Liam and the Fairy Cattle

an Irish legend

Liam and his mother lived by the sea. They had a small white cottage with a pile of peat for the fire outside, and a row of potatoes to eat with the fish that Liam would catch. They had two cows, and Liam's mother would make butter and cheese from their milk. She baked bread and gathered sweet heather honey from the hives at the bottom of the meadow. They did not have much in life, but they were happy.

But then there came a time when ill luck fell on the small white cottage. First the two cows died, one after the other, and there was no cheese to eat. Then the shoals of fish swam far out to sea and Liam would come home empty handed. The potatoes rotted in the ground, and Liam and his mother were hungry all the time.

One day when Liam was wandering along the shoreline he came across two boys throwing stones at a seal.

He shouted at the boys and
chased them away, but
when he went to see if
the seal needed help
it turned its head
once and looked
deep into his eyes
then slipped away
into the sea. As it
dived into the waves he
saw blood on its head.

Three days later
when Liam and his
mother were sitting by the
fire in the evening there came
a knock at the door. There on the
doorstep stood an old, old man leaning
on a staff. His clothes looked wet through and he
had a large cut on his forehead, but his eyes were gentle.

"I am very weary, might I come in and warm myself at
your fire?" the old man asked.

Liam opened the door wide, and bid the old man come
in. His mother pulled up a stool close to the fire, and
warmed up the last of the soup in the pot while she bathed
the wound on his head. He thanked her kindly, smiling at
Liam, and Liam had the strangest feeling he had looked
into those deep brown eyes before. But he made up the fire

for the night and they all slept peacefully until the day.

The old man looked better for his night's shelter, and as he rose to leave he spoke to Liam's mother.

"I have no money to offer you but I would like to thank you for your shelter and food, and I would like to repay the boy here for his kindness," and he turned and looked at Liam with his gentle brown eyes. "I know you have lost your cows so I will tell you where you can find some special cows who will give you milk such as you have never tasted before. Tonight is a full moon and the sea-folk will bring their cattle up out of the sea to graze on the lush green grass that grows just beyond the shoreline."

Liam's mother laughed.

"I have often heard tales of these marvellous cattle, but in all the years I have lived here I have never seen a fairy cow."

"That is because your eyes have not been opened by a touch with the heather that grows on the grave of Fionn who died all those years ago," said the old man and there in his hand he held out a sprig of heather. "Will you let me touch your eyes, and the boy's too?

Then you shall see what you shall see."

Well, Liam's mother felt she had nothing to fear from this kindly old man and so both she and Liam let him touch their eyes with the sprig of heather.

"Now," he said, "you must gather seven handfuls of earth from the churchyard, and then tonight go to the meadow just beyond the shoreline. There you will see the fairy cattle. Choose the seven you like the best and throw the earth onto each one. They will all run back to the sea, save the seven that you have chosen. Bring those seven back home and look after them in your kindly way and they will be with you always. Now I must return from whence I came. Liam, will you walk with me to the sea?" and the old man looked at Liam with those gentle eyes once again.

So Liam and the strange old man walked to the shoreline. One moment they were together on the sand, the next Liam was alone. But when he looked out to sea, there was a seal, looking at him with gentle brown eyes. Then with a ripple, it was gone under the waves.

That night, Liam and his mother did as the old man had bid.

They gathered the earth from the churchyard and made their way quietly down to the meadow. There indeed was the herd of fairy cattle. They were small, no bigger than a sheepdog, and all colours, brown and black and white and brindled. Liam and his mother choose three black, three white and a brindled one, and Liam crept up behind them and threw the earth onto their backs. The rest of the herd scattered back down to the shore and ran into the waves where they quickly disappeared. But the seven in the meadow stood quietly and showed no fear as Liam and his mother led them home.

From that day on, Liam and his mother had a plentiful supply of rich creamy milk. The little fairy cattle would low gently in the byre and were well content with their life on land. But Liam would never let them out to graze when there was a full moon in case the sea-folk came to claim them back.

Wizards and Witches, Giants and Genies

Hansel and Gretel

a retelling from the original tale by the Brothers Grimm

At the edge of a deep, dark forest there lived a poor woodcutter and his wife, a mean spiteful woman, and their two children Hansel and Gretel. The family was very poor and there was often very little food on the table.

One dreadful day there was no food at all and everyone went to bed hungry. Hansel could not sleep, and so it was that he heard his mother talking to his father. "Husband," she said in her thin spiteful voice, "there are too many mouths to feed. You must leave the children in the forest tomorrow."

"Wife, I cannot abandon our children, there are wolves in the forest!" said the poor woodcutter.

But his wife would give him no peace until he had agreed to her wicked plan. Hansel felt his heart grow icy cold. But he was a clever boy and so he slipped out of the house and filled his pockets with the shiny white stones that lay scattered around the house.

The next morning they all rose early and Hansel and Gretel followed their father deep into the forest. He lit them a fire and told them he was going to gather wood and would be back to collect them. He left them, tears falling down his face.

The day passed slowly. Hansel kept their fire going but when night fell, it grew very cold and they could hear all kinds of rustling under the shadowy trees. Gretel could not understand why their father had not come back to collect them, so Hansel had to tell her that their mother had told the woodcutter to leave them there deliberately.

"But don't worry, Gretel," he said with a smile, "I will lead us back home," and there, clear in the moonlight, he showed her the line of shiny white stones that he had dropped from his pocket one by one that morning as their father had led them into the forest. They were soon home where there father greeted them with great joy. But their mother was not pleased.

Some time passed. They managed to survive with very little to eat but another day came when Hansel heard his mother demanding that the woodcutter leave them in the forest again. This time when Hansel went to collect some more shiny pebbles, he found his mother had locked the door and he couldn't get out.

In the morning, their father gave them each a small piece of bread, and then led them even deeper into the forest than before. All day long, Hansel comforted Gretel and told her that this time he had left a trail of breadcrumbs to lead them safely back home. But when the moon rose and the children set off there was not a breadcrumb to be seen. The birds had eaten every last one. There was nothing to do but go to sleep under one of the great big trees and wait to see what they might do in the morning.

All next day they walked and walked, but they saw nothing but more and more great trees. And the next day was the same. By this time they were not only cold and

very hungry but deeply frightened. It looked as if they would never ever be able to find a way out of the forest. But then just as it was getting dark, they came to a little clearing and there stood the most extraordinary house.

The walls were made of gingerbread, the windows of fine spun sugar and the tiles on the roof were brightly striped sweets. Hansel and Gretel could not believe their good luck and they were soon breaking off little bits of the amazing house to eat. But then a little voice came from inside.

"Nibble, nibble, little mouse,

Who is that eating my sweet house?"

Out of the front door came a very old woman. She smiled very sweetly at the children and said, "Dear children, you don't need to eat my house. Come inside and I will give you plenty to eat and you shall sleep in warm cosy beds tonight." Hansel and Gretel needed no second asking. They were soon tucked up, warm and full of hot milk and ginger biscuits and apples. They both fell asleep very quickly. But little did they know they were in worse danger than ever before. The old woman was a wicked witch and she had decided to make Gretel work in the kitchen, and worst of all, she planned to fatten Hansel up so she might eat him!

The very next morning she locked poor Hansel in a big cage and gave Gretel a broom and told her to clean the gingerbread house from top to toe. In the evening, the witch fed Hansel a huge plate of chicken but she only gave poor Gretel a dry hunk of bread. But once she was asleep, Hansel shared his meal with Gretel. And so they lived for many days. The witch could not see very well. So every morning, the witch would make Hansel put his finger through the cage so she could tell how fat he was getting. But clever Hansel poked a chicken bone through the bars so she thought he was still too skinny to eat.

After many days, she grew fed up and decided to eat him anyway, and so she asked Gretel to help her prepare the big oven. The witch made some bread

to go with her supper and when the oven was really hot she put it in to cook. The kitchen was soon filled with the lovely smell of baking bread, and the witch asked Gretel to lift the bread out to cool. But Gretel was clever too. She pretended she couldn't reach the tray, and when the witch bent down inside the oven Gretel gave her a great shove and closed the door with a clang. And that was the end of the witch!

Gretel released Hansel, and together they set off once more to try to find their way home. After all their adventures, fortune finally smiled on them and they soon found the path home where they were reunited with their father who was simply overjoyed to see them again. And what, you might ask, of their mean mother? Well, the poor woodcutter had not had a happy moment since he left the children in the forest. He had become so miserable that she decided there was no living with him. The day before Hansel and Gretel returned, she had upped sticks and left, so that served her right, didn't it?

Amal and the Genie

A Persian fairytale

Many moons ago in ancient Persia there lived a bright young man who knew what was what, and his name was Amal. He was out one day when he had the misfortune to meet a genie. Now sometimes genies can be good news, but this one was in a very bad temper and he was looking for trouble. Amal had to think very quickly. He had no weapons with him, and anyway weapons are no use against genies. All he had in his pocket was an egg and a lump of salt.

The genie came whirling up to Amal, but before he could say anything, Amal yelled at him.

"Genie! You and I should have a competition to see who is the strongest!"

You might think this was very foolish of Amal, but he knew two things about genies. One was that it is always better to take control first, and the second was that genies are not terribly bright. They are fine at conjuring up gorgeous palaces and flying carpets, but they are a bit slow when it comes to basic common sense.

Well, the genie looked at Amal, and then he laughed and laughed. It was not a nice sound, but Amal was not daunted.

"Hah! You don't look very strong," sniggered the genie. "I shall win this contest easily," and he laughed again.

Amal picked up a stone.

"You must squeeze this stone until water comes out of it," he said, handing the genie the stone.

Well, the genie squeezed and squeezed, and huffed and puffed, but, of course, no water came out of the stone. He threw it down in a temper.

"Not possible!" he snapped.

Amal bent down and picked up the stone, and squeezed. And with a scrunching sound, liquid ran down Amal's fingers.

The genie was astonished. And so would you have been if

you had been there. What clever Amal had done was to put the egg in the same hand as the stone, and it was the egg that was broken. But as I said, genies are not terribly bright and this one was no exception. Then Amal said, "Well, I win

that one. But now perhaps you could crumble this stone into powder," and he handed the genie another stone.

Well, the genie squeezed and squeezed, and huffed and puffed, but, of course, the stone did not crumble at all, not even the tiniest bit. The genie threw it down in a temper.

Amal picked it up and squeezed. And as he squeezed, powder fell from his fingers with a grinding sound. The genie was astonished. And so would you have been if you had been there, but you can guess what clever Amal had done. He put the salt in his hand as well as the stone.

The genie was feeling that his reputation was somewhat dented by Amal's performance so he needed to get his own back.

"You are clearly a great and mighty fighter," the genie said to Amal. "I should like to give you a meal to celebrate your achievements. Come and stay the night with me," and he smiled.

But Amal saw the smile, and kept his wits about him. After a dreadful meal (the genie was not a very good cook either) they both lay down to sleep in the genie's cave. Once Amal was sure the genie was asleep, he moved to the other side of the cave, leaving his pillow in the bed to look as if he were still there asleep. Then he watched. As the first light

of dawn filtered into the cave, the genie woke up. He picked
up a huge club and crept over to where he thought Amal
was lying, and he pounded the club down onto the bed,
seven times in all. Then he stomped out of the
cave to fetch some water for his
morning tea.

You can imagine his utter
dismay when, on returning, he
found Amal singing to himself
as he lit the fire.

"Good morning, genie!
I thought I would get
breakfast ready," said
Amal cheerfully. "I hope
you slept better than I did,"
he continued. "Some wretched
insect batted me in the face in
the night, seven times in all."

Well, at this the genie gave a
great shriek and whistled himself
as fast as possible into an old oil
lamp that lay on the floor of the cave. He wasn't seen again
for hundreds and hundreds of years until a young lad called
Aladdin happened to find the lamp. But that is another
story, isn't it?

Snow White and the Seven Dwarfs

a retelling from the original tale by the Brothers Grimm

The queen was sitting at the window sewing, and thinking about her baby who would be born soon. As she sewed she pricked her finger, and red blood fell on the snow by the ebony window ledge.

"I wish that my daughter be as white as snow, as black as ebony and as red as blood," she said to herself, and so it happened. Her tiny daughter had snow-white skin, lips as red as blood and hair as black as ebony, so she was called Snow White. But the queen died and the king married again. His new wife was very beautiful but she had a cold heart, and she did not love Snow White.

Every morning the new queen would look into her magic mirror and say,

"Mirror, mirror on the wall

  Who is fairest in the land?"

and the mirror would always reply,

  "Thou, oh queen,

  Thou art fairest in the land."

So the queen was content. Seven years passed and Snow White grew into a lovely young girl, with her mother's gentle nature.

One morning the queen looked into her mirror as usual, but the mirror's reply filled her with a deep envy.

  "Thou, oh queen,

  Thou art indeed fair

  But Snow White is the fairest in the land."

She ordered her woodsman to kill Snow White. But he could not bear to do such a wicked deed so he hid Snow White deep in the forest. Poor Snow White wandered about until she was utterly weary.

Suddenly, she caught sight of a light through the trees in the distance. It came from a little house with a lantern glowing in one small window. The door swung open at her touch, so she stepped inside. Everything was as neat as a new pin. A scrubbed wooden table was set, with seven plates and seven cups. Seven little chairs were ranged round the fireplace, and along the back wall there were seven little beds, each with a brightly coloured blanket.

There was a basket of logs beside the fireplace, and Snow White soon had a cheerful fire going. She sat in one of the little chairs and before long was fast asleep.

Now the cottage belonged to seven dwarfs and when they came home that evening, they were very worried to discover Snow White fast asleep. They tiptoed round preparing their supper, but as the wonderful smell of stew filled the room, Snow White awoke with a start. She was very surprised to see seven little faces looking at her, but soon she was telling them how she came to be in the forest. They were very angry when they heard about the wicked queen.

"Might I stay with you?" asked Snow White. "I could look after you, and have supper ready for you every night."

The dwarfs were just delighted with this suggestion, and immediately set about making Snow White her own chair by the fireside and her own bed.

Back in the castle, the queen looked into her mirror in the morning, and asked,

"Mirror, mirror on the wall,
Who is fairest in the land?"
But you can imagine her rage when the mirror replied,
"Thou, oh queen,
Thou art indeed fair,
But Snow White with the seven dwarfs does dwell
And she is fairest in the land."
So the wicked queen disguised herself as an old pedlar,

and searched out the dwarfs' cottage. Snow White did not recognise the queen and invited her in.

"Goodness me, you need new laces for your dress," said

the old woman, and she pulled the new laces so tightly that Snow White was unable to breathe.

When the dwarfs came home that evening, they were horrified to discover Snow White lying on the floor as if dead. They lifted her up and, of course, saw the laces. They quickly cut the tight cord and the colour came back to Snow White's cheeks.

"Now you know the queen will stop at nothing," they cried. "You must not let anyone indoors again."

The queen looked in her mirror the next morning, and

went white with rage when it told her Snow White was still the fairest in the land. She disguised herself as a gypsy, selling wooden pegs and combs. Snow White remembered what the dwarfs had said and would not open the door. But the gypsy passed one of the combs through the window, and the minute it touched her hair, Snow White fell down in a faint for the comb was poisoned.

When the dwarfs came home and found Snow White, they immediately suspected the queen. They found the comb and pulled it out, and Snow White sat up, quite recovered. They pleaded with her to be more careful the next morning when they set off for work.

So when a farmer's wife appeared at the door trying to sell apples, Snow White would not even open the window.

"Why, anyone would think I was trying to poison you," said the farmer's wife, who was, of course, the wicked queen in disguise.

"I only want to give you some apples. Look how juicy they are!" and she took a big bite out of one.

So Snow White thought it must be all right and she took the apple. But the queen had poisoned it on one side only, and the minute Snow White took a bite she fell down dead.

This time when the dwarfs came home, there was nothing they could do. Snow White was indeed dead. They could not bear to bury her in the cold earth so they placed her in a glass coffin. They wrote her name on the side in silver and put the coffin in a sheltered part of the forest, and planted wild flowers all round about.

When the queen looked into her mirror the next morning, it gave her the answer she wanted.

"Thou, oh queen,

Thou art fairest in the land."

Years passed. Snow White lay in her coffin, looking as beautiful as ever. The dwarfs watched over her, and one day they found a young prince kneeling by the side of the glass coffin. He had fallen in love with Snow White the moment he had set eyes on her. When the dwarfs saw how deeply the prince felt about their beloved Snow White, they agreed that he take the glass coffin to his palace where he wished to set it in his rose gardens.

As the prince lifted the glass coffin, the piece of poisoned apple flew from her lips, and Snow White opened her eyes. She saw the prince, she saw her faithful dwarfs and she cried, "Where am I? What has happened?"

There was huge excitement as everyone tried to talk at once. The prince wasted no time and asked Snow White to marry him. She agreed as long as the dwarfs could come and live at the palace as well, and they all lived happily ever after.

But what of the queen? She looked in her mirror the morning Snow White and the prince were to be married.

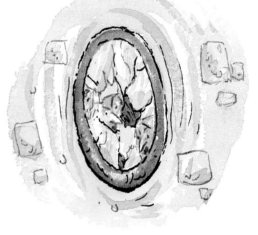

"Mirror, mirror on the wall
Who is fairest in the land?"
The mirror replied,
"Snow White, oh queen,
Snow White who marries
her prince today,
She is fairest in the land."

The queen was so ugly in her rage that the mirror cracked from side to side. And she was never able to look in a mirror ever again as long as she lived.

The Giant who Counted Carrots

a German fairytale

High upon a mountainside there was once a giant who was always very sleepy, and when he went to sleep, he would sleep for hundreds of years at a time. So every time he awoke things had changed a great deal. He spent time as a herdsman, but he did not like being poor. So he went back to sleep. On another visit he spent time as a rich farmer but he found his servants cheated him so he went back to sleep. When he eventually awoke again he wandered down the mountainside to see what he could see.

He came upon a rock pool where a waterfall tumbled down the rocks. A group of laughing girls were sitting dangling their toes in the water. The giant hid and watched. One of the girls was quieter than the others, but to the giant she was the prettiest. Her name was Elizabeth and she was to be married in a few days to the young duke. She and her friends chattered about the forthcoming celebrations as they paddled in the pool, and all the while the giant watched. When they skipped away, his heart grew sad. He realised just how very lonely he was.

He decided to try to win Elizabeth's heart. All through the night he worked. He covered the steep stone under the waterfall with white marble so it sparkled in the clear water. He lined the pool with silver, and filled it with darting golden fish. He covered the banks with rich green grass, planted with sweetly-smelling violets and forget-me-nots and deep blue hyacinths. Then he hid himself again.

219

When the girls arrived they were astonished, but Elizabeth looked thoughtful. She knew that some powerful enchantment had been at work. She wandered to the edge and looked deep into the silver pool, full of the golden fish. And as she looked she heard a voice, whispering, whispering to her to step into the pool. There was a sudden splash, and as her friends looked round in alarm, Elizabeth slipped into the pool. The girls ran over to the pool and looked into the silver depths. In vain they tried to find her. When they went home and told the young duke, he came with all haste to the pool. All the giant's adornments had vanished. The waterfall fell over steep and black rocks, the silver lining and the golden fish had disappeared from the pool, and there was not a single flower to be seen. Sadly, the duke went back to the palace and nothing would cheer him.

Meanwhile Elizabeth found herself in the giant's garden. He begged her to stay with him and be his queen, but she told him she loved the duke and would not forsake him. The giant hoped she would forget the duke, but as the

days passed he saw that she grew pale and sad. He
wondered how he could cheer her, and change her mind.
Then he remembered his magic staff. Whatever it touched
would turn into any animal he wished for. He gave the staff
to Elizabeth and for a few hours she was happy as,
first a kitten then a dog then a canary appeared
thanks to the staff. But it was not long before
she grew silent again.

Now the giant grew very good
carrots, and he was very proud of
his carrots. He pulled some for
supper and Elizabeth said she
had never tasted such
delicious carrots in all her life,
which was true.
So the next day, the giant took
Elizabeth out into the fields
round the castle where the carrots
grew. As far as the eye could see
there were carrots, row upon row
of them. Elizabeth asked the giant
how many there were, but he
couldn't tell her that at all. So she
begged him to count at least one
row, and as he began counting she quickly drew the staff
out from under her cloak and touched a black stone that
lay on the ground. It turned into a black horse with great

hooves that pounded the earth as Elizabeth mounted its back and fled down the valley away, away from the giant.

The very next day, Elizabeth married her duke and they lived happily ever after. The lonely giant went slowly back to his garden, and fell into a deep sleep. Many hundreds of years passed and still the giant never awoke. In time grass and plants and trees grew over the slumbering giant, and still he slept on. Over the years the mound that was the sleeping giant became known as Giant Mountain, and so it is still called today. So beware if you see great rows of carrots on a mountain side, you might be very near a sleeping giant!

The Mermaid of Zennor

a Cornish legend

The bell was ringing, calling the villagers of Zennor to Sunday service. It was a simple little granite towered church, built to withstand the wild winds and weather that could roll in from the sea. Matthew Trewella stood in the choir stalls and looked at the new bench he had been carving. It was nearly finished and wanted only one more panel to be carved.

As the voices of the congregation rang out in the hymns, a sweet pure voice was heard. A voice that no one had heard before. When the villagers turned to leave at the end of the service, there at the back of the little church stood the most beautiful woman any of them had ever seen. Her dress was made of soft rustling silk, at one moment green, the next blue, like the sea. Round her neck she wore a gleaming necklace of pearls, and her golden hair fell down her back almost to the floor.

As Matthew walked out, the woman placed her hand on his sleeve.

"Your carving is beautiful, Matthew."

Matthew blushed and turned his rough cap round and round in his great red hands, his deep blue eyes wary.

"Why, thank you ma'am," he managed to stutter before he fled out of the church. Where the beautiful lady went no one quite saw.

The next day Matthew was hard at work, carving the decoration of leaves that went round the edge of the bench when he heard the soft rustle of silk. There stood the woman again.

"What will you put in the last panel, Matthew?" she whispered. And she smiled into his deep blue eyes. Matthew sensed a strong smell of the sea in the tiny church as he bent to get up off his knees but when he looked up again, there was no sign of the woman.

The next Sunday the lady was in church again. She looked deep into Matthew's eyes as she sang the hymns, and when he walked slowly out, as if in a dream, she was waiting for him.

"Will you carve my image in the last panel, Matthew?" she asked and her voice was gentle and sighing like the withdrawing tide on a shingle beach. Matthew's deep blue eyes gazed far over her head, out towards the sea, but he did not reply. Only the schoolmaster and his wife noticed that the seat where the woman had sat was wet, wet with sea water. But they said nothing.

Time passed, and every Sunday the woman came to church. Matthew seemed like a man in a dream, his eyes always looking out to sea. The final panel was still not finished on the bench. November came, and with it the mist curled up from the sea. Night after night a light was to be seen late in the church. The gentle sound of wood chipping drifted out with the mist, but no one ventured into the church.

It was the parson who

discovered the finished bench when he went in to open up the church one morning. The church floor was wet, wet with sea water. The stub of a candle stood among a great pile of wood shavings on the floor. The final panel of the bench was the best Matthew had ever carved. It was a mermaid, long hair falling down her back, the scales of her great fish tail in deep relief. She looked almost alive.

Matthew Trewella had not slept in his bed that night, nor was he ever seen again in Zennor. The mysterious woman never came to church again. The schoolmaster and his wife never talked of the wet seat. Only the fishermen would shake their heads as they sat talking on the winter's evenings. They would talk of the mermaid they had seen off the coast, and of the young man with the deep blue eyes who was always swimming by her side.

The Seven Ravens

a fairytale from Poland

There was once a poor widow who had seven great sons and a daughter. The daughter, Anne, was a good girl, but the seven brothers were wild as the hills. One day the widow was baking a blackberry pie. As she rolled out the pastry the whole noisy troop came shouting into the kitchen.

"Blackberry pie!" they yelled. "When will it be ready?"

"When it is cooked," she said crossly. "Let me finish then we can all eat." But the boys just ran about the hot kitchen, pushing and shoving each other and leaving great muddy bootmarks all over the clean floor.

"Oh, can't you be quiet! I wish, I wish you were ravens instead of great noisy boys," she cried. But then her eyes widened in horror as the boys shrank, and feathers covered their arms. Their mouths turned into beaks, and with seven deep croaks they flew out of the door. Anne rushed to the window, but the ravens were already out of sight. Together mother and daughter sat weeping, and not even the smell of burning pie could rouse them.

But the next day Anne said to her mother, "I am determined to find my brothers and bring them safely back home."

So she set off with nothing but her needle and thread

and scissors in her pocket. She walked and walked and came across a curious little house in the woods. It was made of silver, and the woman who opened the door was dressed in a long silver robe. But she was not friendly.

"I am all behind today, and my husband will be home soon. There is no supper ready, and I have to mend his cloak," she said all in a rush.

"I could mend the cloak," said Anne taking out her needle, "and then you can cook the supper."

Well, the woman was delighted and opened the door wide. Anne sat quietly in the corner and with the tiniest stitches ever mended the beautiful cloak. When the husband, who was also dressed all in silver, came in he was very impressed with Anne's work, and invited her to join them for supper which was the most delicious roast chicken.

The silver man asked Anne where she was going so she told them the whole story of her brothers.

"Perhaps we can help you," said the silver man. "We are the moon's helpers and she sees most things on earth. I will ask her if she knows where your brothers are."

As the wife cleared the table after supper, she gave Anne the chicken bones.

"Keep these in your pocket, you never know when they might come in useful," and Anne did so.

When the silver man returned the next morning he told Anne that the moon had seen seven ravens flying round the Amber Mountain. When Anne asked him where the Amber Mountain was he told her to follow her nose until she could go no further. Anne thanked the silver couple and set off once again, her nose very firmly in front.

After several days she came to a halt. There in front of her was the Amber Mountain, its sides steep as glass. Anne did not know what to do, but then she remembered the chicken bones. She pushed one into the surface of the mountain and stood on it. Then she put the second bone in a little higher, and stood on that, and so she slowly, slowly climbed to the very top of the mountain. And there she found seven sad-looking ravens. They were her brothers! But there was also an evil old witch sitting there too.

"Well, my dear, your brothers are under my spell, and the only way you can release them is by remaining silent for seven years. Not one single word or you will lose them for ever," and with an evil cackle she flew off.

Anne climbed down the mountain, and when she reached home her mother was delighted to see her. But Anne could tell her nothing. Four years passed in silence until one day Anne was out gathering firewood when a royal hunting party came through the wood. The prince was very struck by Anne's quiet ways, but of course he couldn't get a word out of her. Thereafter he came by every day, and at length asked her to marry him. She smiled her acceptance but never a word did she utter.

Three more years passed, and the prince and Anne had a baby son. Now the queen had never really approved of her son marrying such a poor girl, however pretty she might be, and she never lost an opportunity to make mischief. One day she rushed into the prince and accused Anne of trying to poison the baby. The prince was horrified but, of course, when he asked Anne if she had done such a terrible

thing, she was unable to reply. So he sent her to the dungeons, and told her she had three days to explain herself or she would die.

The three days passed with Anne still not uttering a word. On the third day, she was brought out into the courtyard where everyone waited to see what would happen next.

Suddenly there was a great flapping of wings and seven

ravens landed in a circle around Anne. It was her brothers, and in a blink of an eye there they stood, restored to human shape. Well, you can imagine what a lot Anne had to tell! They all talked into the night. The queen had somehow gone missing, but no one seemed to mind too much. The seven brothers went to collect their mother, and when they all came back together the prince promised her that she would never have to do a day's work again!

The Twelve Windows

From 'Told Again' by Walter de la Mare

There was once a princess who lived alone with her father the king, the queen having died many years before. The princess was wise and gentle and loved her father very much, so much so that the king dreaded the day when the princess would marry and leave him alone in the empty palace. But she had promised she would never marry until she met a man who would have three chances to hide himself in the palace so cleverly that she could not see him. Now you might think this was not so difficult but the princess had witch's eyes and she could spy out the smallest thing like an ant or one tiny daisy on the palace lawn. She had a special room at the top of a tower in the palace which had twelve windows that the princess could look out of to practise her great skill.

Many princes and handsome young men came to court the princess but all failed to hide themselves well enough. Now there was a swineherd who would watch the princes and the handsome young men come and go, and after a while he thought he might just as well try himself to see if he could win the hand of the princess. When he arrived at the palace gate, the guards just laughed at him, but the watchman who was passing at the time thought the young swineherd had an honest face. So he lent him a cloak of green velvet, and the swineherd was ushered into the princess's rooms.

Straightaway she saw that he had an honest face, but she also saw his poor clothes under the cloak, and she saw his heart beating against his ribs. She wished him luck, and gave him an hour to hide. The swineherd went down, down deep into the palace dungeons and hid himself under a pile of straw. When the hour was up, the princess climbed up into her special room and looked through the first window. She could see no sign of the swineherd. She looked through the second window. She could see no sign of the swineherd. But then she looked through the third window, and there she could see him, lying under the straw. The princess was sorry as she realised that the young swineherd was the first of the many young men who had come to court her that she actually liked.

The next day, the swineherd went to the palace fish pond and, taking a deep breath, he plunged to the bottom of the pond and hid under the roots of the graceful water lilies. He waited and waited, his lungs bursting. The princess climbed up into her special room and looked through the first window, then the second, the third, the fourth and the fifth. There was no sign of the swineherd, and the princess found she was pleased. She looked through the sixth and the seventh and the eighth. There was no sign of the swineherd and the princess found she was delighted. But then she looked through the ninth, and she saw the swineherd crouched in the pond, under the roots of the water lilies. The princess found she was full of sadness.

The young swineherd realised he was up against some powerful witchcraft, so that night he went to seek out his friend the white fox. He told her all about the princess and her witch's eyes, and he also told the fox that he had fallen in love with the princess. The fox just nodded and told him to get a good night's sleep. She woke him in the morning before it was light. When the swineherd was washed and dressed, the fox touched him with the tip of her tail, and he turned into a beautiful white mountain hare. Then she turned herself into an old woman and, taking the hare in her arms, she walked to the palace and stood by the garden gate.

The princess was walking in the palace gardens, her face sad as she thought of the swineherd who today faced his last chance at becoming her husband. She saw an old woman standing by the garden gate, with a white mountain hare in her arms. The hare looked so beautiful that the princess could not resist going up to stroke its fur. The old woman who, of course, was really the clever fox, gave the hare who, of course, was really the swineherd, to the princess. The princess was amazed by the beauty of the hare and by the softness of its fur, but when she went to give it back, the old woman had disappeared. The princess placed the hare on her shoulder and together they climbed

the stairs to the room with the twelve windows.

The hare crept round under the princess's hair as she looked out of the first window. There was no sign of the swineherd. She looked out of all the windows until she came to the twelfth. There was no sign of the swineherd. With a beating heart she went to look out of the last window. She so wanted not to see the swineherd. She looked and looked again. She could not see him! The one thing witch's eyes cannot do is see behind them, and so the swineherd had won the hand of the princess. The hare darted down the stairs while the princess was still crying with delight, and ran out of the palace to where the fox was waiting. She touched the hare with the tip of her tail and there stood the swineherd once again.

He thanked the fox profusely and than ran back to the palace as fast as ever he could. There he found the princess

standing in the garden looking everywhere for him. They went to see the king, and the whole story came out. The princess and the swineherd said they loved each other. The swineherd said he did not want to live anywhere else in the land. So the king did not lose his daughter. The princess married a man she really liked. The swineherd gained everything from just having a try. The white fox was invited to the wedding, and they all lived happily ever after.

Sleeping Beauty

a retelling from the original tale by Charles Perrault

 Long, long ago, when fairies were still able to grant wishes, there lived a king and queen who wanted, more than anything in the whole world, to have a baby daughter. When their wish was finally granted and a beautiful tiny princess lay in her cradle, the king and queen decided to have a great candlelit party to celebrate. They invited the twelve most important fairies in the land and a great many other people besides.

As well as the thousands of glittering candles, there were golden tables piled high with all kinds of delicious food, and the royal orchestra played their most cheerful tunes. The twelve fairies all lined up to present their christening gifts to the tiny princess. Their gifts were those that only a fairy can give: beauty, kindness, grace, honesty and the like. The princess smiled happily in her cradle as one by one the fairies tiptoed up.

The eleventh fairy had just promised the princess a sweet singing voice, when there was a great roll of thunder and all the candles flickered out. There stood quite the most wicked fairy anyone had ever seen. She was dressed all in black, her long straggly hair was black and her eyes, glittering in rage, were as black as the crow's feathers. Her voice was like a saw as she screeched, "How dare you not invite me to the party! I too have a gift for the little princess," and she smiled a not very nice smile. "Because you have forgotten me, my gift is that when the princess is sixteen she shall prick her finger on a spindle and die!" and with a horrid laugh, the wicked fairy disappeared with another clap of thunder.

As the candles were hastily relit, everyone started talking at once. Then a quiet voice was heard over all the hubbub. It was the twelfth fairy.

"I cannot undo this wicked spell," she whispered, "but I can decree that the princess will not die. She will instead fall into a deep sleep for a hundred years," and all the fairies slipped away leaving the court in despair.

The king, of course, immediately ordered that all the spinning wheels in the land were to be burned. After a while, everyone grew less frightened, and as the princess grew up into the most lovely girl, the wicked fairy's prediction slipped from most people's memories.

On her sixteenth birthday the princess went exploring. At the top of a tower she did not remember seeing before, she found an old woman, sitting at a spinning wheel.

It was, of course, the wicked fairy in disguise. The princess was fascinated and, as she bent forward to look at the cloth, her hand caught the sharp spindle and she immediately fell to the ground as though dead. With a swirl of smoke and a nasty laugh, the wicked fairy disappeared.

Everyone else in the palace fell asleep at the same moment. The king fell asleep with his ministers, the queen and her maids fell asleep in her dressing room. The cook fell asleep in the kitchen in the middle of baking a cake, the groom fell asleep as he fed the horses in the stables and even the little linnet the princess had in a golden cage by her bedside fell asleep on its perch. A great high thorn hedge grew up and soon the palace was completely hidden. Time stood still and all was silent.

Many, many years passed. The tale of the sleeping princess spread far and wide, and many came to try to find her. But no one could get through the thorn hedge. And so after even more years, people forgot what lay behind the hedge.

Then one day a handsome prince came riding through the woods, and as he reached the thorn hedge, thousands of pink roses burst into bloom. The prince walked forward, and a path appeared leading through the hedge towards the palace. It was a hundred years to the day since the princess had pricked her finger. The prince was astonished by the sight that met his eyes. Everywhere people lay asleep, frozen in the midst of whatever they had been doing when the spell caught them.

The prince climbed the tower, and there he found the princess, looking as lovely as ever. He bent over and kissed her, and immediately the spell was broken. The king and his ministers carried on just where they had left off. The queen chose which dress she wanted to wear and the maids brushed her hair. The cook put her cake in the oven and the

groom led the horses out into the courtyard. And even the little linnet in her golden cage sang a joyful song.

As for the princess. . . ! Well, she and the prince had fallen in love with each other on the spot, and were married the very next day. They all lived happily ever after, and the wicked fairy was never ever seen again.

Rapunzel

a retelling from the original fairytale by the Brothers Grimm

nce upon a time there lived a man and his wife who for years and years had wanted a child. One day the wife was looking sadly out of the window. Winter was coming but in the next door garden, which was surrounded by a huge great wall, she could just see rows and rows of delicious vegetables. In particular, she could see a huge bunch of rapunzel, a special kind of lettuce. Her mouth watered, it looked so fresh and green.

"Husband, I shall not rest until I have some of that rapunzel growing next door," she whispered.

The husband clambered over the wall and quickly picked a small bunch which he took back to his wife. She made it into a salad, and ate it all up. But the next day, all she could think of was how delicious it had been so she asked him to pick her some more.

He clambered over the wall again, and was picking a small bunch of the rapunzel when a voice behind him hissed, "So you are the one who has been stealing my rapunzel!"

When he spun round, there stood a witch and she looked very angry indeed. The husband was terrified, but he tried to explain that his wife had been desperate for some fresh leaves for her salad.

"You may take all the leaves you require then, but you must give me your first child when she is born," smiled the witch, and it was not a nice smile. The husband was greatly relieved, however, for he knew that there was little chance of his wife ever having a daughter so he fled back over the wall, clutching the bunch of rapunzel. He did not tell his wife of his meeting with the witch for he thought it would only frighten her, and he soon forgot all about his adventure.

But it all came back to him when nine months later his wife gave birth to a beautiful baby girl. No sooner had she laid the baby in her cradle, than the witch appeared to claim the child. The wife wept, the husband pleaded but nothing could persuade the witch to forget the husband's awful promise, and so she took the tiny baby away.

The witch called the baby Rapunzel.
She grew into a beautiful girl with long,
long hair as fine as spun gold. When she
was sixteen, the witch took Rapunzel
and locked her into a tall tower so no
one would see how beautiful she
was. The witch threw away the
key to the tower, and so whenever
she wanted to visit Rapunzel she would
call out, "Rapunzel, Rapunzel, let down your hair,"
and Rapunzel would throw her golden plait of hair
out of the window at the top of the tower so the witch
could slowly scramble up.

Now one day it happened that a handsome young
prince was riding through the woods. He heard the
witch call out to Rapunzel and he watched her climb
up the tower. After the witch had gone, the prince came
to the bottom of the tower and he called up, "Rapunzel,
Rapunzel, let down your hair," and he climbed quickly up
the shining golden plait. You can imagine Rapunzel's
astonishment when she saw the handsome Prince standing
in front of her but she was soon laughing at his stories.
When he left, he promised to come again the next day, and
he did. And the next, and the next, and soon they had fallen
in love with each other.

One day as the witch clambered up Rapunzel

exclaimed, "You are slow! The prince doesn't take nearly as long to climb up the tower," but no sooner were the words out of her mouth than she realised her terrible mistake. The witch seized the long, long golden plait and cut it off. She drove Rapunzel far, far away from the tower, and then sat down to await the prince. When the witch heard him calling, she threw the golden plait out of the window. Imagine the prince's dismay when he sprang into the room only to discover the horrible witch instead of his beautiful Rapunzel! When the witch told him he would never see his Rapunzel again, in his grief he flung himself out of the tower. He fell into some brambles which scratched his eyes so he could no longer see.

And thus he wandered the land, always asking if anyone had seen his Rapunzel. After seven long years, he came to the place where she had hidden herself away. As he stumbled down the road, Rapunzel recognised him and with a great cry of joy she ran up to him and took him gently by the hand to her little cottage in the woods. As she washed his face, two of her tears fell on the prince's eyes and his sight came back. And so they went back to his palace and lived happily ever after. The witch, you will be pleased to hear, had not been able to get down from the tower, so she did NOT live happily ever after!

Teeny-Tiny

an English folk tale

Once upon a time there lived a teeny-tiny old woman. She lived in a teeny-tiny house in a teeny-tiny street with a teeny-tiny cat. One day the teeny-tiny woman decided to go out for a teeny-tiny walk. She put on her teeny-tiny boots and her teeny-tiny bonnet, and off she set.

When she had walked a teeny-tiny way down the teeny-tiny street, she went through a teeny-tiny gate into a teeny-tiny graveyard, which was a teeny-tiny shortcut to the teeny-tiny meadow. Well, she had only taken a few teeny-tiny steps when she saw a teeny-tiny bone lying on

top of a teeny-tiny grave. She thought that would do very well to make some teeny-tiny soup for supper so she put the teeny-tiny bone in her teeny-tiny pocket and went home at once to her teeny-tiny house.

Now the teeny-tiny woman was tired when she reached her teeny-tiny house so she did not make the teeny-tiny soup immediately but put the teeny-tiny bone into her teeny-tiny cupboard. Then she sat in her teeny-tiny chair and put her teeny-tiny feet up and had a teeny-tiny sleep. But she had only been asleep a teeny-tiny time when she woke up at the sound of a teeny-tiny voice coming from her teeny-tiny cupboard. The teeny-tiny voice said, "Where is my teeny-tiny bone?"

Well, the teeny-tiny woman was a teeny-tiny bit frightened so she wrapped her teeny-tiny shawl round her teeny-tiny head and went to sleep again. She had only been asleep a teeny-tiny time when the teeny-tiny voice came from the teeny-tiny cupboard again, a teeny-tiny bit louder this time. "Where is my teeny-tiny bone?"

The teeny-tiny woman was a teeny-tiny bit more frightened than last time so she hid under the teeny-tiny cushions, but she could not go back to sleep, not even a teeny-tiny bit. Then the teeny-tiny voice came again and this time it was even a teeny-tiny bit louder. "Where is my teeny-tiny bone?"

This time the teeny-tiny woman sat up in her teeny-tiny chair and said in her loudest teeny-tiny voice, "TAKE IT!"

There was a teeny-tiny silence, and then a teeny-tiny ghost ran out of the teeny-tiny house, down the teeny-tiny street, through the teeny-tiny gate into the teeny-tiny graveyard – with the teeny-tiny bone clutched very tightly in its teeny-tiny hand! And the teeny-tiny woman never took even a teeny-tiny walk there ever again!